Fair Dalliance:
Fifteen Stories
by
Yoshiyuki Junnosuke

Fair Dalliance:
Fifteen Stories
by
Yoshiyuki Junnosuke

Compiled and edited
by
Lawrence Rogers

Kurodahan Press
2011

Fair Dalliance: Fifteen Stories by Yoshiyuki Junnosuke
Compiled and edited by Lawrence Rogers

All stories are copyright Yoshiyuki Junnosuke, and translated
with the permission and encouragement of Honme Mariko.

Translation copyright © 2011 Lawrence Rogers, except as otherwise indicated for individual stories. First publication information begins on page 175.

FG-JP0029-L36
ISBN-13: 978-4-902075-39-7
ISBN-10: 4-902075-39-3

KURODAHAN PRESS
Kurodahan Press is a division of Intercom, Ltd.
#403 Tenjin 3-9-10, Chuo-ku, Fukuoka 810-0001 JAPAN
www.kurodahan.com

Table of contents

Preface

THIS COLLECTION HAS COME into being out of the conviction that the short stories of Yoshiyuki Junnosuke, if they were made accessible in English between the covers of one book, would certainly be appreciated and enjoyed abroad as they have been in Japan. The prolific Yoshiyuki has left us a vast body of literature, a feast of short stories, novels, novellas, essays on a wide range of topics, translations from English, and light fiction whose function is simply to entertain. An edition of his complete works published in 1983, eleven years before death stilled his pen, had 17 volumes of his writing.

Junnosuke was born in the spring of 1924, the first child of what would become a gifted clutch of Yoshiyuki children. The Yoshiyuki family had lived in provincial Okayama, but moved to Tokyo three years later as his father Eisuke pursued his career—ultimately abandoned—as a writer in the Dadaist tradition.

Junnosuke himself had become seriously interested in writing by his late teens. The story goes that when his home burned in one of the air raids on Tokyo in the final months of World War II he fled the flames with only his Debussy records and some fifty poems he had written in a notebook. He entered what was then Tokyo Imperial University, but seems to have devoted more time to writing for coterie magazines than to his classes, and, we are told, never even paid his tuition. He dropped out and began editing what he himself later called a third-rate scandal sheet. His first short story, published elsewhere, came out in 1950, and his course was set when he won the opportune Akutagawa Prize with his short story "Sudden Shower" (Shūu) in 1954. He went on to win all the major literary awards over the years, and, more importantly, to develop a substantial and loyal readership. After he became an established writer, he himself would become a member of the same prestigious selection committees.[1] At the time of his death in 1994 Junnosuke was certainly the best-known member of the talented Yoshiyuki clan, which was no mean accomplishment itself, since his sister Kazuko had, and still has, a respected career in acting on the stage, in films and on television, and also as a writer. His youngest sister Rie, who died in 2006, was a published poet and short story writer. As if that were not enough renown for one family, his mother Aguri, who had been a beautician, became a household name in 1997 when NHK, the government-supported network, telecast the long-running and very popular *Aguri* dramatic series based on her life.

Unfortunately, Yoshiyuki's constitution was never as robust as his literary imagination. He was bedeviled by poor health from childhood. He contracted typhoid fever in his teens and later tuberculosis and other lung afflictions; he suffered from depression, asthma, assorted allergies, psoriasis, and a cataract in one eye. He died of liver cancer after a two-and-a-half year struggle with the disease. His sister Kazuko wrote that his health was such that one naturally expected him to be feeling unwell on any given day. She recalled looking forward to visits with him during his frequent stays in the hospital, approaching each as a kind of picnic and, together with their mother, bringing him a basket of his favorite foods.[2]

1 Yoshiyuki was also one of a number of prominent authors who were asked to testify for the defense in the obscenity trial centering on a short story attributed to the writer Nagai Kafū, a cause célèbre in the 1970s and an indication of the respect Yoshiyuki enjoyed in the writing community.

2 "Ani to watashi," *Gunzō*, vol. 49, no. 10, October 1994, p. 188–189.

Initially, at least, the asthma served a vital purpose: it rendered him unfit for the military during the desperate last year of the war. This serendipitous rejection was not seen by Yoshiyuki as a missed opportunity, as one suspects a similar rejection was by his contemporary, Mishima Yukio. Neither did Yoshiyuki's often-described apathy toward the jingoism of wartime Japan evolve, as it did for many young writers of his generation, into a public embrace of pacifism or Marxism once the war was over and authoritarian Japan dismantled. In this apolitical sense Yoshiyuki stood apart from many writers of his generation.

In an article written well into his career Yoshiyuki complained that his work continued to be misunderstood by some: "There is a hardy tendency to misread my works as naturalist realism. . . . I consider my work now to be 'internal realism,'" a term he said he appropriated from the writing of Paul Klee. As to influences, he wrote that when he was young he read extensively the literary icons of Imperial Russia—Chekhov, Gogol, Pushkin, Mikhail Lermontov—and acknowledged his debt also to Thomas Mann and Arthur Schnitzler. Yoshiyuki said he was less impressed with Anglo-American writers, whose literature he simply identified as "works introduced in the wake of the defeat." He wrote that many of these efforts he set aside as unreadable. The short stories of Henry Miller, which he translated and admired as stories he himself might have written, were the definite exceptions, of course. Miller's novels, on the other hand, struck him as "brimming with an enormous energy" that he found overwhelming. In fact, when a special edition of a literary journal devoted to his work was published—there were a number of these over the years—his antipathy toward the idea of possible Anglo-American influence prompted him to ask that such an article be dropped.[3]

---

3 "Jisaku ni tsuite no kansō iroiro," *Kokubungaku: kaishaku to kanshō*, vol. 40, no. 11, October 1975, pp. 6–10.

In his fifties Yoshiyuki experienced a severe case of psoriasis, a painful affliction that nonetheless gave him the opportunity to record—or create—the machinations of the old quack doctor in the clearly autobiographical sketch "Katsushika Ward" (Katsushika), the final story in this collection. It is a curious piece sprinkled with place names encountered in driving from one side of Tokyo to the other; published in 1980, a time when travel by one's own car was becoming less of a novelty, at least for the more affluent, the story may well have been found informative, as well as entertaining, by a new driver. One is reminded of the *sharebon* fiction of the Edo era set in the urban pleasure quarters which, besides the pure entertainment of a story line, also provided practical advice on travel, accommodations, and customs. And despite its setting, the eros of the *sharebon* was implicit or understated, as it is in much of Yoshiyuki's fiction.

Tasking an anthologist to point out his or her favorite story is fair, if problematic. The pieces published here, though only a small sampling of Yoshiyuki's extensive oeuvre, have qualities that I think are fairly representative of his four decades of work. In "The Man Who Fired the Bath," for example, Yoshiyuki amuses with one of his more guilt-ridden neurotics, a hapless—and nameless—soul who, in shifting his attentions from one woman to another certainly has our interest, if not our sympathy, as he absurdly seeks to destroy the dreaded red bundle. The first story in this collection, the poignant "My Bed Is a Boat," attracted favorable attention when it was first published early in Yoshiyuki's career. The respected economist and Yoshiyuki aficionado Hidaka Hiroshi, writing in 1977, considered it not only outstanding amongst Yoshiyuki's own works, but a masterpiece of postwar Japanese short fiction, "the very best of the lyrical."[4]

---

4 "Nedai no fune ni tsuite" in *Yoshiyuki Junnosuke zenshū*, supplement 3, Kōdansha, 1985, p. 116.

Yoshiyuki was apparently a complex personality, and perceptions of him vary depending on the observer, though friends apparently saw in his psyche certain traits that marked the stereotypical edokko, or child of Edo, in the Tokugawa era. He was said, for example, to have had a love of gambling and a willingness to bet on just about anything: whether the next person coming through the door would be wearing glasses, or the chance of rain before morning. To some he was a man inevitably in high spirits, the loquacious cut-up at the party. For others, such as the younger writer Murakami Ryū, Yoshiyuki was a shy man: "Every time I met him I had the feeling that I was learning how vital it is to have a sense of embarrassment."[5]

I regret that I never met Yoshiyuki-*sensei*, but I did exchange several brief notes with him, mostly regarding the copyright for his short stories. The first exchange was in the mid-eighties on permission to translate and publish his "Hydrangeas" (Ajisai). He generously—and doubtless hopefully—advised that since he was not that adept at English I should translate it as I saw fit, at my own pace and to my own satisfaction. He himself had published several translations from English, so I took his reluctance as simple modesty. Several years later, when I asked for permission to translate and publish the quirky "The Battle of the Clays" (Nendo gassen), he expressed mild surprise—but not disappointment—that I should have been interested in such an offbeat piece. "Clays" is certainly a departure from his bordello and bar scene stories, but it is part of the substantial and intriguing Yoshiyuki subgenre of grotesque surrealism, which we clearly see in this collection in "Three Dreams" (Yume mittsu) and hints of in the pocket piece "The Flies" (Hae).

Yoshiyuki's work as an English-to-Japanese translator was intermittent and limited. He translated the stories of the once-banned Miller and the comedic novelist Kingsley Amis, and the seventeenth century Japanese of Ihara Saikaku into the

---

5 "Inga na koto ni sainō ga aru," *Gunzō*, ibid., p. 203.

modern language. Yoshiyuki professed an ignorance of pre-modern Japanese literature and claimed an almost "immunological rejection" of its grammar, but perhaps we should not be surprised that he made an exception for the bawdy Saikaku.[6]

Whatever his inclination toward Saikaku and the pleasure quarters of Edo-era Japan, in the twentieth century Yoshiyuki recreated prosaic reality with a bald honesty that is harder to come by in Saikaku's stories idealizing the circumstances of all those "Women Who Loved Love." In one piece, "Japanese Handball" (Temari), a Yoshiyuki-like character meets a prostitute several times over a period of years. He recalls his shifting impressions of her changing circumstances. "She was wearing a starched dress, so her thin body looked like a dried fish thrust into a paper bag." Six years before he had gone to her room. "He bared the spare, flat chest that he remembered" from yet an earlier encounter. But this time he sees that she is pregnant: "He completely lost his desire to make love to her." As the piece ends we see a little girl bouncing her ball, a child Yoshiyuki does not identify, but one that confronts us as a question mark. In another story, "Perfume Bottles" (Kōsuibin), a former companion-for-hire informs the hero that she has syphilis, and asks matter-of-factly how his most recent blood test went. But of course Yoshiyuki's corpus is not all failed birth control and the threat of disfiguring disease. He can also be appreciated for a subtle drollery that surfaces unexpectedly as in "A Certain Married Couple" (Aru fūfu), when the narrator relates the difficulty of redeeming those "call girl coupons."

We should also note Yoshiyuki's occasional use of foreign nursery rhymes in his stories. The literary critic Takahashi Hiromitsu has found eight short stories in Yoshiyuki's oeuvre that exploit children's verse.[7] Takahashi sees a similarity between these and the prose-poetry of the Heian period known as *uta-monogatari*, in which an episode, usually amorous, is

6 *Kokubungaku*, pp. 8–9.

7 Takahashi Hiromitsu, *Yoshiyuki Junnosuke: hito to bungaku*, Bensei Shuppan, 2007, pp. 91–94.

capped by a waka poem integral to the prose. While Yoshiyuki's selected verse is at a good remove contextually from the
surrounding prose, the technique is a clear, if distant, echo of
the *uta-monogatari*. Four stories in this collection have such
rhymes: "Twins" (Sōsei), "Perfume Bottles," "Something Unexpected" (Fui no dekigoto), and "My Bed Is a Boat" (Nedai no
fune), in which the narrator awakes in the bed of a male prostitute.[8] Implanting nursery rhymes in such a context seems at
least counterintuitive, but in fact they can serve as effective, if
provocative, transitions.

Finally, given the skein of the erotic that threads its way
through his work and the fact that Yoshiyuki is a writer very
much of the I-novel tradition, we should not be surprised—
nor incurious—about the reality that Yoshiyuki seems to have
lived a rather colorful love life (though some may question the
aptness of the term "love" in all instances). What was not expected was the publication after his death of four books by
four different women describing, by their own lights, their
own relationships with Yoshiyuki.[9] That a man of letters who
largely made his living chronicling relationships with women
should, in the end, be the object himself of such accounts is
not without irony.

The fifteen short stories translated here are presented in
order of publication in the original Japanese, beginning with
"My Bed Is a Boat," published in 1958, early in Yoshiyuki's
writing career, and ending with "Katsushika Ward," which appeared in 1980. Only four of the stories have been previously
translated into English.

I want to thank Edward Lipsett, publisher of Kurodahan
Press, for expanding the body of Yoshiyuki's work in English
and to thank him and the copy editor Nancy H. Ross for their
helpful comments. I would also like to thank the copyright

---

8 According to Takahashi, the Japanese translations Yoshiyuki used are all from
Sekai dōyōshū, Fuzambō, 1924, Saijō and Mizutani, translators.

9 Perhaps the most imaginative title of the four books was *The Deep Cave in the Dark
Room Where Yoshiyuki Junnosuke and I Secluded Ourselves.*

holder, Honme Mariko, for giving permission for this collection and Corinne Quentin for invaluable assistance in making it possible. I also owe a debt of gratitude to Donald Richie for his unflagging encouragement over a number of years and for generously agreeing to write the Introduction. And I am grateful for the steadfast support of my wife, Kazuko Fujihira, ever-willing smiter of linguistic ambiguity.

The editor is pleased to acknowledge the translating labors of Hiroko Igarashi, who teaches Japanese at the University of Hawai'i at Hilo, and William Matsuda, a Ph.D. candidate at the University of Hawai'i at Manoa currently studying in Kyoto, Japan.

Personal names in these translations are given in the Japanese style, surname first.

Lawrence Rogers
Kurtistown, Hawai'i
rogers@hawaii.edu

Introduction

YOSHIYUKI JUNNOSUKE (1924–1994) WAS one of Japan's fin-
est postwar writers, yet this is not generally acknowledged. In
Japan he is famous but popularly regarded as a writer of mere
erotica. In the West he is almost entirely unknown. Only one
major work, *The Dark Room* (Anshitsu, 1970) and a few short
pieces have been translated.[1]

Yet of him no less than Mishima Yukio wrote: "The deli-
cacy of Yoshiyuki's language and sensibility is probably more
subtle and sophisticated than that of any Japanese writer since
[World War II]. . . . The lyricism of Yoshiyuki's writing is semi-
neurotic and, by restricting his subject, he is able to convey a
deeply sensual experience in a world as confined as a bathtub."[2]

The subtly explored bathtub is Yoshiyuki's preferred subject,
which is sex, a narrow but deep concern. A passage from *The
Dark Room* indicates this interest. "[T]ake a room at an inn,
strip off, converse for a while in sounds that [are] not speech,
then have a bath and go our respective ways . . . (it was I who
determined the pattern, the women just went along with it.)"[3]

As for intimacy, Yoshiyuki wrote in the 1958 short story "In
Akiko's Room," "I said nothing, but carried on a long, intricate

1 *The Dark Room*, John Bester, translator, Kodansha International, 1975.

2 Geoffrey Bownas and Yukio Mishima, *New Writing in Japan*, Penguin, 1972, p.
20–21, Geoffrey Bownas, translator.

3 *The Dark Room*, p. 84.

conversation with her body."[4] In thinking about something as individual as her name, however, he realizes that it has slipped his mind. "Often enough, it too disappeared entirely, leaving only the reality of her body" (*The Dark Room*). [5]

The reality of the body—as though that is the only reality that there is. This at any rate is the only one that the narrator of "In Akiko's Room" allows himself, and since most of his women are prostitutes it is the only one that they are allowed at all. Hence "I felt a sense of kinship with all the women who stood in the doorways of those tasteless, garishly painted houses. I was at home with them." And when the two of them, whore and client, got together "it seemed to me that the two of us . . . were exchanging the look of accomplices."[6]

Looking around further, the narrator ("semi-neurotic" or not) finds parallels to his own situation. "When two attractive women embrace, they exist in a purely sensual world. No pregnancy, no domesticity, just the play of the senses. A woman is far closer acquainted than a man with the subtleties of the female body. A woman can bring another woman's body to fever pitch in much the same ways as her own. The two bodies with their swelling breasts touch each other not as ivy embraces the tree, but as ivy entwining with ivy. . . ."[7]

Since this is something the narrator himself wants (no pregnancy, no domesticity, just noncommittal connections based entirely on sex), he finds his ideal in such infertile relationships. A transvestite gets an erection with the narrator, who then says: "With the state you're in there's no reason you couldn't do it with a woman." To which the answer is: "'I am a woman, dear. I wouldn't get this way with another woman.' I was baffled: was it laughable or sad that when she was trying to

4 *Contemporary Japanese Literature: An Anthology of Fiction, Film, and Other Writing Since 1945*, Howard Hibbitt, editor, Alfred A. Knopf, 1983, p. 403; Howard Hibbett, translator.

5 *The Dark Room*, p. 128.

6 *Contemporary Japanese Literature*, p. 408

7 *The Dark Room*, p. 88.

be her most feminine her body became its most masculine?"
("My Bed Is a Boat"). Laughable or sad? One of the indications of depth in Yoshiyuki's work is that he can never make up his mind. Life in all of its parallels and paradoxes is never one single, simple, convenient thing. Rather, it is lots of things, many of them opposed to each other. As in this passage from *The Dark Room*:

"You're supposed to be an erotic writer, you see. Actually, only a certain proportion of readers think that: the rest see you as plain sexy."

"What's the difference between 'erotic' and 'sexy'?"

"'Erotic' has class and 'sexy' doesn't. A very important distinction."

"I see."[8]

Yoshiyuki always asks questions like this because his is a quest for some kind of authenticity. Indeed, if the body is the only reality, is simple sex enough? Maybe not. In "Sudden Shower," the short story that won Yoshiyuki the Akutagawa prize and launched his literary career, the narrator remembers the feeling that came over him "at the idea that he had touched the heart of a prostitute, someone so difficult to move in that she offered her body so readily."[9]

It is as though the narrator senses under the plain surface (sex) the throbbing, horrid, wonderful authenticity he is searching for. Again and again Yoshiyuki offers parallels—things hidden under things. For example, in the city the ground is paved over "making it something of a problem to actually see the naked earth" ("Hydrangeas"). Here, the ordinary world of humans is contrasted with the naked world of nature just beneath—something to be observed. This idea expands from narrative to narrative. "Its color was dark, somber and wet, not the sort of color one encounters in everyday life. What was normally hidden from view deep within the mammalian

8 Ibid., pp. 16–17.
9 *New Writing in Japan*, p. 118.

body lay out on the pavement, as though it had been dumped into the street . . ." ("I Ran Over a Cat.").

To be compared with "You slap the belly of a blue-backed fish down on a concrete floor and it splits open . . . its guts pop out . . . the thin membrane around the gut is slimy with fat, and reflects the light of the sun, glistening with all the colors of the rainbow, like machine oil floating on a puddle" ("Something Unexpected").

And to be interiorized, as in the 1965 short story "Scenes at Table." "The act of eating always has about it a sense of exposure of explicitness. . . . When you open your mouth, a red mucous membrane appears. You shovel in the meat of beasts, waggle your jaw, then shift the food to your throat. The flesh there jerks up and down, and the saliva-soaked mush drops to the stomach. The stomach is ready with a yellowish liquid that it pours onto the food while beginning to roil the mass. The mush is eventually passed from the stomach to the bowels where, at the end of a tract many meters in length, there is tightly packed waste matter that has yielded its nutriment, that is, the feces. The sense of naked explicitness involved in eating a meal somehow resembles the sex act."[10] As the literary critic Miyoko Docherty has said, "Yoshiyuki employs sex as a medium to examine the nature of human existence."[11] Under its seductive surface lies the truth, just as under the word on the page lies the meaning.

The author's life was unusually full of reading and writing. There were lots of books in his past. His father, Yoshiyuki Eisuke (1906–1940), was also a writer, an avant-garde poet, a man who finally lost faith in literature and threw away his library, all except the three books he had published. His son found these unreadable, decided to forge a style more durable, and kept his faith in literature.

---

10 In *Japan Echo*, vol. 12, 1985, p. 44, Geraldine Harcourt, translator.

11 *Kodansha Encyclopedia of Japan*, Gen Itasaka, editor in chief, vol. 8, Kodansha,1983, p. 351.

One of the ways in which he did so was by keeping his fiction autobiographical, as though what had actually happened was the only reality. For example, for a time he worked on a scandal sheet, *Modern Japan* (Modan Nihon), and stayed with it for the six years it took for the magazine to expire. From that time on this poor publication began appearing in his own writings.

"I was supporting myself as a reporter on a scandal magazine" ("In Akiko's Room"); "In my capacity as a reporter for a third-rate weekly news magazine . . ." ("Something Unexpected"); "I . . . was on the staff of a third-rate popular magazine" (*The Dark Room*).[12]

The scandal sheet experience was important because *Modern Japan* gave the author his first education on the darker side of society and reinforced his antipathy to conformity. During his schooldays he had much resented the growing militaristic atmosphere of the place and the patriotic fervor of his classmates. When the war ended he was equally against joining anything like communism or Marxism. He felt the same about these new varieties of fanaticism as he had about the nationalistic ardor of others during the war.

Remembering his avant-garde father, he once wrote that he himself was motivated by a similar Dada-like desire to undermine the conventionally accepted definitions of beauty and ugliness, good and evil. He also discovered the work of another older writer who shared these ideas, Thomas Mann, particularly in his "Tonio Kröger." In it Yoshiyuki discovered Mann's contention that happy people are those who do not get involved with literature, that the unhappy ones are those sensitive people whose hearts are stolen by the art. Yoshiyuki said he identified strongly with this. He wanted to purpose a fairly unhappy literary career at a time when society was moving in the direction of a cheerfully shared militarism.

---

12 *The Dark Room*, p. 13.

About his own literary style Yoshiyuki once said: "I believe only in clarity," and then quoted from "Tonio Kröger:" "If you attach too much importance to what you have to say, if it means too much to you emotionally, then you may be certain that your work will be a complete fiasco."[13] About this style, translator Maryellen Toman Mori has written that "[c]entral to his ideal was the concept of balance. He sought to identify and to realize the perfect balance between subjectivity and objectivity, between emotional involvement with his material and dispassionate rendering of impressions. He concurs with Thomas Mann, who stressed the necessity of cultivating an 'inhuman' side in order to avoid producing a 'pathetic, sentimental, plodding, over-serious, incoherent, bland, boring, trite' work. . . . [Yoshiyuki's] controlled manner of expression creates a tone of mild irony and aloofness, but at the same time evokes a delicate pathos."[14]

As though in counterweight to Mann, Yoshiyuki also discovered another foreign mentor. This was Henry Miller, an American expatriate who disliked social regimentation as much as anyone and did something about it in books as sexually free as *The Tropic of Cancer*. Strongly drawn to the picaresque liberties taken, Yoshiyuki began translating several of Miller's works, and the matter-of-fact sexuality of the American's work inspired the complete sexual acceptance of the Japanese author.

As in the creation of any literary style, there were many other influences. In *The Dark Room* the narrator remembers a foreign novel he read when in high school and was much impressed by. It was about a gangster whose front teeth had been replaced with gold, whose young body was pocked with scars left by bullets. "The kisses of his golden mouth were cold, and the fingertips of the women who held his body would slip into

---

13 "Tonio Kröger," David Luke, translator, in *Death in Venice, Tonio Kröger, and Other Writings*, Continuum, 1999, p. 21.

14 Mori, Maryellen Toman "Enmeshed in Illicit Liaisons: Yoshiyuki Junnosuke and His Imagery," *Japan Quarterly*, vol. 28, no. 1, Jan–Mar 1981, p. 89.

the holes in his back."[15] The narrator has forgotten the name of the book, but it is obviously *Belle de Jour*, the Joseph Kessel novel now better known as the basis for the Luis Buñuel film. All three men were in some ways much alike, and it is interesting to contemplate a Buñuel adaptation of, say, Yoshiyuki's *The Dark Room*.

At the same time that he was reading Thomas Mann, Henry Miller and Joseph Kessel, Yoshiyuki was also reading Japanese literature, particularly the *gesaku* writings of the Edo period (1600–1868). The term refers to popular fiction of the time and originally meant "written for fun" rather than for enlightenment or for governmental purposes.

As a genre it is characterized by its flippant attitude and a certain style that, says Wolfgang Schamoni, "combines facetiousness of tone with elaborate structure . . . [a] synthesis of the demotic and the erudite." It is also "characterized by wordplay, parody of earlier works, and intricate formal construction at the expense of the story itself. . . . behind the jocular facade there can at times be detected a sense of passive opposition to the values of feudal society"—a near perfect fit for Yoshiyuki.[16]

The major *gesaku* writer was Ihara Saikaku (1642–1693), and Yoshiyuki was soon "translating" him into contemporary Japanese and writing about the experience. In *The Dark Room* the narrator even quotes from Saikaku's *Five Women Who Loved Love*: "Every woman has a part that no man can refuse. Even the Buddha himself would get a little involved."[17] In addition, Yoshiyuki was rediscovering the earlier work of Natsume Sōseki, itself much influenced by the *gesaku* style, and revisiting the works of Nagai Kafū, that master of Edo nostalgia and himself possessed of one of the most perfect of literary styles. And for those who treasure the sheer eccentricity of the *gesaku* writer, Yoshiyuki's voice can be heard on the soundtrack

15 *The Dark Room*, p. 88.

16 *Kodansha Encyclopedia of Japan*, vol. 3, p. 28.

17 *The Dark Room*, p. 144.

of the "erotic" anime *One Thousand and One Arabian Nights* (Sen'ya ichiya monogatari, 1969).

Scholar Howard Hibbett has observed how "the cool, polished surface of his fiction faithfully reflects a world of mingled frivolity and futility."[18] These qualities are particularly displayed in Yoshiyuki's humor: "Choku used to be a pimp . . . Since Choku was a university graduate, however, making a living this way was not the least bit unusual" ("A Certain Married Couple"); "The many live sex shows he had seen all followed a formula, much in the style of the exercise programs on morning radio" ("Japanese Handball"). And we are told in one of his early short stories, "Are the Trees Green?": "The ending for a man in love is always bad."[19]

Or perhaps that last is not meant to be funny. That the ending of a man in love is always bad could indeed be the moral of *The Dark Room*, which is also the archetypal Yoshiyuki story. The middle-aged narrator has arranged his life as he wants it. This includes a number of compliant women, always ready to have him drop in for the night. He thus avoids all responsibility and all emotional investment. If he misses the emotional heights he also avoids the emotional depths. He has, however, neglected one fact—things change. Restricted to one woman he finds himself hovering on the edge of that hateful involvement which we might also call love. "By now I needed her. It's her body you need, I tried telling myself . . . but somehow I felt it didn't account for everything."[20] The dark room waits.

If it is the picaresque amorality of the Yoshiyuki story that intrigues, it is this movement toward the undesired resolution that moves. It is this that makes his work feel so authentic. Promiscuity, sheer numbers, is finally not enough. As the narrator observes in the brief 1974 story "Three Policemen," "Worry about women is a concomitant part of all men's lives. Lots of

---

18 *Contemporary Japanese Literature*, p. 401.

19 *The Shōwa Anthology: Modern Japanese Short Stories: 1929–1984*, Van C. Gessel and Tomone Matsumoto, editors, Kodansha International, 1985, p. 165.

20 *The Dark Room*, p. 158.

men are crying inside."[21] But this is not "not enough" because of any moral code or social convention but simply because we, as humans, are not enough. Yoshiyuki has the ability to lift the stone and look under it and to do so (as Mishima noted) in the most sophisticated and subtle of manners.

Donald Richie
Tokyo

---

21 In *Seven Stories of Modern Japan*, Leith Morton, editor, University of Sydney East Asian Series Number 5, Wild Peony, 1991, p. 53; Hugh Clarke, translator.

My Bed Is a Boat

寝台の舟

Translated by Lawrence Rogers

LET ME TELL YOU a story that goes way back.

At the time I was almost completely burned out. I was teaching at a girls' school and just barely able to make ends meet.[1] The school building stood by the sea. Between the train station and the building there was a cavernous tunnel that had been dug through solid rock, and at the entrance was a sign: *Rocks occasionally fall here, so please keep an eye out overhead.* In fact, the walls inside the tunnel were inevitably wet with seeping water, and sometimes when I was walking through it I would hear the sound of rock that had broken off crashing to the ground and echoing around me. It was a tunnel that somehow seemed slapdash, that didn't quite permit you the assurance that no large, life-threatening rock would break off and end your life. To be sure, however, if the tunnel had not been there, I would most certainly have abandoned my commute to the girls' school long before.

The expanse of sea visible from a school window was a soiled smalt, and the many girls' eyes directed at me as I stood at the lectern inexplicably lacked the shine of cleverness, offering only a stagnant sullenness. However the wind that blew off the sea and the delicately shifting air that enfolded the girls'

---

1 Yoshiyuki taught part-time at a girls' high school in 1946, the year after the war ended, a time of food shortages and widespread malnutrition.

young bodies in the classroom filled my heart with good feeling. At the same time, the damp, chill air in the tunnel and the occasional echo of falling rock caused every cell in my body to tense.

So even though I was almost completely worn out, I could expect recovery through a petty, trivial incident of some sort. This I knew. I was waiting for an insignificant occurrence that would remind my cells of when they had been filled with the juices of youth and would validate this conviction; yet nothing happened.

I felt a tightness in my chest whenever I saw the mailman. Yet there was never any mail for me. And I myself sent mail to no one.

One night while idly scrutinizing the rows of books in a second-hand bookstore in town—and because I was almost completely exhausted—I began to feel sentimental. I bought a small, well-thumbed collection of Western nursery rhymes.

When I returned to my tatami room I tossed the book into a corner and crawled into bed. As I lay down I felt that countless cells were shriveling by the second; I fell fast asleep. That deep sleep assailed me day after day. The book of nursery rhymes lay abandoned in the corner of my room just where I had tossed it.

One night I extended an arm from my futon, raised myself up on my elbow, and drew the small, well-thumbed book to me. The book fell open to a page and my gaze dropped to a poem called "My Bed is a Boat."[2]

My bed is like a little boat;
Nurse helps me in when I embark;
She girds me in my sailor's coat
And starts me in the dark.

2 From Robert Louis Stevenson's *A Child's Garden of Verse*, published in 1885. Yoshi-yuki used the Japanese translation by the poet and lyricist Saijō Yaso (1892–1970), but changed the order of the poem's four quatrains.

I read just the first stanza then, swimmer-like, thrashed my arms and legs about several times in my forlorn bed, a wry smile on my lips, and fell asleep.

> All night across the dark we steer;
> But when the day returns at last,
> Safe in my room, beside the pier,
> I find my vessel fast.

The two heavy curtains were not fully closed, letting the morning light shine through the gap between them. I awoke on a large bed. I awoke on an expanse of bed that seemed to take up more than half the room, a bed bigger than a double bed. In a room I'd never seen before. For a moment I couldn't bring into focus the place where I lay. A figure in a scarlet under-kimono lay at my side. The neck emerging from the collar of the wrap, a neck from which makeup had flaked off, was, indisputably, a man's neck. The morning light, intruding through the gap in the curtains, shone upon the many follicles where the hairs of the beard had been plucked out and on the male oil that oozed from the face.

I looked around the room. There was a large three-mirror vanity that seemed to take up almost all the remaining space unoccupied by the bed. On the vanity were row upon row of glass bottles of all shapes and sizes filled with countless liquids: red, green, milk white, and some clear. These were concrete manifestations of the obsession of the human being lying at my side to transform himself into a woman. They were not the devices a man would use to change himself into a woman simply as an eccentric taste of current fashion. Here and there amongst the glass bottles standing in disarray lay metal implements, bent and twisted into sundry shapes. These seemed to me to be devices for applying makeup; the precise use I could not fathom. To me the three-mirror vanity was a tableau of vivid, unforgiving despair.

"I hate that I don't have breasts!" the man at my side who last night had identified himself as Misako had moaned. I recalled the vivid despair. That the curtains were parted now was for "Misako" a major oversight, most certainly.

I got out of bed and took another careful look at the neck, which clearly exposed to view its characteristic maleness, then brought the curtains together. In the now-dim room the conspicuous size of the bed struck me anew.

What had I done last night?

I had had some money in my pocket, an uncommon situation. A colleague at the girls' school had passed on some moonlighting work, and that was the source of the money. The work in question was translating a manual for farming tools written in English. As I converted into Japanese script the proper usage of various grubbers attached to tractors to break up soil, from time to time I would be confronted with terminology unclear to me. Uneasy in the extreme that I had indeed been able to till this plot of land, I nonetheless handed over my translation, hoping for the best. Fortunately the manuscript had turned itself into money.

So I went out on the town that night, drank and got myself drunk. A woman in a kimono hailed me on a dimly-lit street and took me to her room. We went in and chatted there, and for a good while I didn't realize the body wrapped in Japanese attire was a man's. What gave rise to doubts was the overabundant charm of her bearing and the excessive warmth of her solicitude.

My gaze fell on the Adam's apple, artfully concealed under the collar of the kimono.

"Aha," I said, "you're not a woman."

"My name is Misako," she replied, then silently regarded me for a moment before speaking again. "You want to leave?"

"I'll stay."

I had no taste for sex with another man, but I was curious. Besides, I didn't want to get up and go back to my room at this point. "Misako" was talkative now.

"Stay over. I'll tell you all about myself. Not every single thing I do for someone is for real, I'll tell you. There're any number of ways to fool 'em. There's the real thing, and there're ways to fool people. I'll show you the whole bit."

I'd been reduced to impotence, however, and had no use for either the real thing or ways to fool people. She was annoyed and blurted out that I wasn't able to function just because she wasn't a woman, but whether that was the reason wasn't all that clear even to me; I had been strongly stimulated by the human being who was next to me in bed. Misako had pressed her body against mine. Her hard sexual organ had bumped knife-like against the relaxed expanse of my stomach. I had assumed an asexuality in her, so I was caught off guard. My automatic response was to stick out my hand and touch it. What I felt was hard and vigorous.

"You meanie!"

She shifted her body away from me and evaded my hand. What burned fiercely within me was, as I had expected, curiosity.

"With the state you're in there's no reason you couldn't do it with a woman."

"I'm a woman, dear. I wouldn't get this way with another woman."

I was baffled; was it laughable or sad that when she was trying to be her most feminine her body became its most masculine? Or perhaps she felt a hidden joy that I could not glimpse: becoming a woman and being pinned down, her various muscles manfully tensing as she collided with a tensed body of the same gender. That's what I was ruminating on.

It was then that the pressure I felt against my abdomen weakened and a husky voice breathed into my ear. "I'd like to cut it off and throw it away!"

In that instant I sensed a woman in the body next to me. Or it might be better to say I felt passion in that vivid despair. But I was still impotent, doubtless because of the alcohol. My impatience came to the fore. When I realized that, I smiled wryly: Well, what the hell.

At the same time she was turning sentimental and started telling me the story of her life. Hearing someone's life story got

— 5 —

me in a sentimental mood as well, but this particular tale was extremely boring. As she scooped up handfuls of her life for me, a lot of things must have run through her fingers. A life's story that should have been singular extended not an inch beyond the realm of my expectations.

The telling went on and on. My sense of duty to listen disappeared and I turned raffish. I reached out and touched her flat chest and the now-shrunken sexual organ. I was bored. Around me was the expanse of sheet over the huge mattress. I was sleepy. I realized that I would soon drift off.

A stanza from that children's poem, "My Bed is a Boat," rose indistinct in my brain. I slipped into sleep as I slowly threaded my way through the verse, word by word.

And sometimes to bed things I take,
As prudent sailors have to do;
Perhaps a slice of wedding-cake,
Perhaps a toy or two.

That's the kind of night the previous night had been for me. And now I awoke to the light of morning. I closed the gap in the curtains to block the sunlight and left the room, Misako still in bed asleep.

I got my train, got off at my station, and went through the tunnel. There before me was the smalt expanse of sea. I made my way to the girls' school before it, then walked into my classroom wherein the bodies of so many girls were arranged as neatly as stones on a *go* board.

I GOT A PHONE call at the girls' school by the sea from Misako. She had pestered me for my business card, so I had left one with her.

She asked me to come to her room and visit. I hesitated; the telephone was not located in a suitable place where I, a teacher at a girls' school, could engage in a verbal to-and-fro. I promised to go see her.

Once in her room I sat on the large bed, my tie unloosened, and listened to the tiresome story of her life. The telling was tedious, but the gentle grace of her evident concern affected me deeply. That gentleness got to me, worn and weakened as I was.

And that gentleness was extraordinary. The gentleness that she, a man, projected in order to comport herself as a woman struck me as something unique. I couldn't quite put my finger on it, but it seemed to me this was because, completely worn down, she was attempting to reinvigorate her last years as a woman, and what emerged from this was the gentleness. This idea gradually came into sharper focus when she showed me a nude photo. It was a photo of her, a three-quarters shot, from mid-thigh up. In it she was smiling, her head tilted slightly and her arms crossed in front of her chest.

"What do you think? You can only take me for a woman, right?"

It was all I could do not to ask how many years ago the picture had been taken. The outline of her face and her body gently curved, so that one almost mistook the figure for a woman's. Gentle curves had just about disappeared from the body of the woman I now saw before me. This was inevitable. It is nature's way that a female becomes more feminine as her girlish appearance fades and the characteristics of the male become more pronounced the further he gets from boyhood. This inevitability, however, because it is inevitable, had certainly worn her down that much more.

I casually looked behind me. There was just a white wall. I shifted my gaze, looking about the room. Everything—the large bed, the massive three-mirror vanity, the heavy cloth curtains—appeared to be things that had once cost real money, but they were no longer new, their colors a bit faded. The look of the whole room told of a life that had once been luxurious. The old phrase "the chamber of a cherished imperial favorite who was now falling out of favor" came to mind. But I knew that her renown would hold considerable cachet for some even now.

I sat across from her in the room as she focused her singular gentleness on me.

"It was during the war. You wouldn't have been strolling around the pond there? I wonder if I didn't meet you."

"I doubt it."

"Then it must have been someone else. You look just like him. I offered up my virginity to him."

Because of her singular gentleness, I took the talk that we had, even the parts that were extremely sentimental and smacked of artifice, to be words from her heart. There's the old saw that a drowning man will clutch at a straw, and it came to me that I was now that straw; for an instant I felt an unsupportable fatigue. After that day my curiosity vis-à-vis her turned into something else. Something different. To say that it was compassion is to overly narrow the gap between the two of us. And it's not like the hidden tangle of emotions that conspirators have. Perhaps you might even say that a gentleness had insinuated itself into the feelings I had for her.

And yet I had no desire to visit her in her room. Nonetheless, when she phoned the girls' school by the sea, I agreed to go there.

The man in the office came to inform me.

"Sir, you've a phone call."

He studied my face, an unpleasant look in his eye.

"It's a call from someone with a voice like a woman," he said, "and like a man."

I had not intended to work at the school indefinitely. And seeing the look in that man's eye, I sensed the time to quit was near.

IN HER ROOM I was—and continued to be—impotent. My heart accepted her, but my flesh harshly rejected her. In spite of which, whenever she phoned I set off for her room.

When I would set a determined course in the direction of her room and be walking along the street, there was an instant when I would suddenly feel that the juices of youth had filled every cell in my body. When I entered her room, however, I was, yet again, impotent.

From time to time irritation would get the best of her and she would poke me.

"You've no problem with women!" she would say, her voice husky. "Listen, I'm a woman! Please think of me as one."

She was absolutely right. Had she actually been a woman I most certainly would have been able to extricate myself from my impotence, even without the entanglement of emotion. When I heard her talking like that my mood would darken, and I would decide that I was being cruel and could not bring myself to look at her. When I heard that voice of vivid despair, I felt I was committing a crime.

"I'll give you an injection," she said one night, regarding me carefully. "Then I'm sure there'll be no problem."

Imprudently, I nodded. She drew fluid from an ampule into a hypodermic syringe and broke off the top of another ampule with a file.

"Let's double the dose to make sure it works," she said, working the file, head down. I gazed at the bent head and the hard line of her cheekbone and the depilated hair follicles around her mouth and was instantly gripped by fear. She was completely worn down. There was now scarcely a drop of young and seductive blood left in her veins. And even if they had been filled to bursting with the blood of a vigorous young man, her veins were for her the veins of death.

I realized she was in a situation where she might have no qualms about confronting death. The image suddenly came to me of a dear friend who had been poisoned in a murder-suicide the previous year, the unsuspecting victim of a widow—an older woman—who had slipped poison into his glass.

I nonetheless entrusted my bare arm to Misako. My mindset was offhand, enervated.

The syringe was for subcutaneous injection. Yet she had taken a towel and tightly wound it around my upper arm. She then began probing for a vein in the crook of my arm with the fine point of the needle.

I held my arm absolutely still. The vein eluding the needle tip, she poked about in the muscle again and again. Sharp pain repeatedly assaulted my arm. My thought in this betwixt state was that I was punishing myself.

At long last the point of the needle found its vein, and the fluid surged into the arm. I tensely waited for the physical transformation.

She took the hypodermic she had withdrawn from my arm and, without sterilizing it, filled it with another dose and poked about in her own arm until she found a vein. Head lowered, but eyes turned up to watch me carefully, she pressed the plunger of the syringe embedded in her arm, where several rivulets of blood now trickled.

I waited. Apparently, however, a dose that would harm me was not circulating in my system, nor did lust thrust itself to the fore. I waited some more. There was no change, however.

As soon as I realized this, I was overcome by an intense fatigue. I knew that I must never again set foot in that room.

"How's it?" she asked. "Is it working?"

A faint pink flush circled her eyes, which now twinkled more than usual.

"Not at all," I sighed in reply.

I RESIGNED MY TEACHING job at the girls' school by the sea shortly thereafter.

And I did not return to the room of the male prostitute Misako.

When I told the students, lined up in their proper rows in front of me, that I was resigning, their eyes, as always, held that sullen, stagnant light. That's how it seemed to me, yet there were several girls who would miss me.

As I was cleaning out my desk in the faculty room the day I left the school, three girls approached. The girl in the middle wordlessly proffered a bouquet of flowers she was holding. The cellophane wrapped around the flowers glistened a dingy white. I was suddenly overcome by shyness. And the image of me having to board the train carrying that bouquet crossed my mind. Without thinking, I pushed the flowers back into the girl's arms.

"I've no use for these," I heard myself say. "Thanks, but I've no use for them."

When I saw the girls' befuddlement, however, I reconsidered. I accepted the bouquet and stuck it in a vase in the faculty room. The flowers were yellow roses. Leaving the flowers at the school, I departed. And I never went back.

Thereafter I shut myself up in my room and ate nothing but dumplings made of wheat flour. Thus keeping the wolf from the door, I assumed that a suitable line of work would eventually present itself.

That was the situation when one day the postman surprised me with two envelopes. One was from the girls' school by the sea and contained my scant severance pay. The other was from the girl who had given me the floral bouquet; the gist of it was as follows:

"I understand, sir, the reason you did not want to accept the bouquet of flowers. I later realized that yellow roses symbolize infidelity. Thus you most certainly found accepting the flowers distasteful. Please forgive me, *Sensei*."

I laughed out loud for more than a little while. Even after the humor of it had passed I made a point of laughing.

And my head was filled with images of the questioning eyes directed at me by the man in the office of the girls' school by the smalt sea and of the room with the huge bed and the three-mirror vanity.

I got up, clutching the envelope with the money, and stood motionless on the tatami. I was considering a visit to the room of the male prostitute Misako.

I decided I would go to that room, my first visit in a long while, and bring a token gift of some sort. I visualized the disordered mix of glass bottles, large and small, before the three mirrors. I would buy a bottle of perfume and make my visit. I began noticing foreign perfumes in town. They were quite expensive. Buying one of those would wipe out my limited severance pay. And I would have to go on eating the dumplings. Nonetheless, I would buy the perfume and take it with me.

I was sure that when I saw her smiling face my heart would fill with gentleness. Perhaps I would then make an attempt to see her as a woman. She would press her body against mine. Yet I would still be unable to respond to her. Be that as it may, she would become a woman, and between our embracing bodies her organ would achieve a vigorous fullness.

I might well become annoyed when that happened. Clutching the bottle of perfume, I would extend my arm and pour its contents on her penis as it soared upward vainly. I would drain the bottle, down to its last drop. I would pour it out until the penis, engorged with its power and the symbol of her having become a woman, was wrapped in an obscuring mist of high scent.

Captivated by this fantasy, I stood there in my room for some time.

However I made no effort to walk to the door; I simply sat down where I was on the tatami. Then I crawled into the futon that still lay nearby. The book of Western nursery rhymes that I had tossed into the corner of the room remained where I had left it. It was covered with a layer of pale dust.

Recalling a stanza in it, I was drawn in the light of day into a deep sleep.

At night I go on board and say
Good-night to all my friends on shore;
I shut my eyes and sail away
And see and hear no more.

Japanese Handball

手鞠

TRANSLATED BY HIROKO IGARASHI AND LAWRENCE ROGERS

WHEN KENJI SAW THE figure of a woman illuminated by the lights of the city at the shuttered entrance to a department store, his immediate response was to disappear into the crowd. But the woman quickly caught his eye before he could look away and drew up to him, holding him with her gaze.

She was wearing a starched dress, her thin body like a dried fish thrust into a paper bag. She carried a cheap plastic handbag. Overall, however, she had a trim look, a not unappealing appearance. The way she had intentionally applied blush to her sunken cheeks was the same as when he had first seen her six years earlier, but her red cheeks now projected the melancholy suggestion of age. Nonetheless, she couldn't have been over thirty-five.

She walked toward him, her shoulders rounded and her flat chest concave. A smile, goodness itself, creased her face. He was no match for that smile. He had tried to avoid her because of her circumstances: she was still working the streets. He had no other reason for running away from her.

She approached him.

"How about it?" she whispered, "Want to keep me company?"

"Didn't we decide some time back that I wouldn't be going with you?"

"I don't mean like that. I couldn't make it if I was still doing that." She went on, saying she was now making a living by soliciting customers for erotic films and live sex shows.

He was not that much aroused by such shows anymore, but he was curious about her life these days. He turned to the man he was with.

"How about it? Wanna go?"

His companion was enthusiastic. Following the woman, the two men entered one of the backstreets of the town. The pavement gave way to a black dirt road, narrow and naked, and here and there slushy.

It came to him then that he could no longer find obscure pleasure in entering clandestine places. He recalled in an instant his feeling when he saw a sex film for the first time. He was stunned at the fact that so much time had passed.

It had been the second summer after the end of the war. A college student was putting on a show, renting the small basement of a building and two reels of erotic films. The student wanted to make money. The tickets were absurdly expensive. He charged the same price that you would pay today to see such a movie. Kenji wanted, almost desperately, to see the movies. Being acquainted with the organizer, he could get a discount; yet he also needed to sell his English dictionary to get in. His major was English, so his desire was clearly extraordinary.

The door to the small basement had been securely locked from the inside. The projector started running. Fair flesh and flesh a bit darker began to intertwine on the blurred screen. There was the sound of pounding on the door.

"Open up! Open the door!"

Tension immediately filled the basement room. The voice, almost a scream, called out again, and the sound of the thumping fist grew louder.

"That's him. What a damned nuisance!"

There was muttering, and a student stood up and headed toward the door. Kenji realized that the man shouting was the law student who had helped organize the show. The latecomer's voice was plainly fraught lest he miss even one frame. His tone was raw, embarrassingly so. Kenji was astonished that the student could yell like that, and, at the same time, he understood deep down his anxiety.

Two short films, each one about ten minutes, were played back to back, and the show was over. Kenji's eyes were dazzled when the lights abruptly returned. A student two rows in front of him looked back at his friend and smiled. The other's smiling face filled his field of vision. A greasy sweat oozed from the young man's flushed face. Kenji guessed the student grinned with the intention of showing the world an adult grin that said, "Hey, that was something, wasn't it!" However that intention failed and only laid bare the inexperience of raw youth. Kenji stared with animosity at the pustules on the student's forehead. Yet even if he himself might laugh, the fact was he didn't have the confidence to display any other expression. He continued to sit rigid in the chair, back straight.

It was several months after that show that he first met the woman who was now, twelve years later, walking before him, her shoulders bony and her back bent. She had caught his eye as he was walking in the district in the northeast corner of the city, where brothels lined the street.

Twelve years before he had seen her as fresh-faced, a woman unable to shake the aura of the amateur. He had decided he would stay the night in her room. He soon regretted choosing her, however. Sex films had been something new to him, but not a woman's body. He was disappointed by the ample crook in her neck, her flat chest, the meager moisture. And when she smiled her cool, insouciant features gave way instantaneously. Incredibly, her face became an ordinary face, one of pure goodness. After she felt at ease with him she readily smiled at even his trivial utterances. And she would laugh wildly, her laughter a donkey-like bray.

Looking at her fragile frame, it occurred to him that the reason she could endure the intense physical labor with such a body must have been because of this laughter. He decided fatigue would pass through her unimpeded because of her optimistic soul. He then abandoned his initial plan to spend the night beside a lovely beauty, and passed his time giggling with her instead.

SOME SIX YEARS LATER he chanced on her in a brothel district in the center of the city. She still remembered him. As always, she enticed him with that smile of goodness itself.

"Oh, hello! It's been a long time, hasn't it? Why don't you come to my room?"

It was a casual invitation, one that did not suggest it had been a rather long six years. He had thought of her with fondness. And at the same time he also remembered her body. He didn't feel the urge to go to her room.

In those days there was a woman he liked in a brothel in the district, so he often set off for the quarter. The gaunt woman seemed not to be able to attract customers and was always standing in front of the house. Whenever she saw him she called out.

"Hi! Why don't you come in?"

She sounded as though she had already resigned herself to him not accepting her invitation. However, inevitably smiling cheerfully, she would extend her invitation instead of a conventional greeting.

"Hi! Why don't you come in?"

He would take from his pocket chocolates and other candy he had won at a pachinko parlor and put these in the palm of her upturned hand. "Well, take care," he would say, and leave. This became his way of greeting her.

However one night she buttonholed him, her approach different this time. She said she had been standing in front of the brothel all evening but hadn't had a single customer. She asked him to buy her services to save face with the brothel.

He entered her room at last, the first time in six years. He took off her nightclothes as she lay beside him. He bared the spare, flat chest that he remembered. But below that her body presented an unfamiliar contour. The profile of her body from her chest, over her abdomen, and to the creased flesh above her thighs, rose up, swollen at her belly.

"Are you pregnant?" he asked.

"Yes."

"Inconvenient in your line of work, isn't it?"

"Right. I was thinking of going to the doctor, but somehow time went by, and here I am."

"I'd guess it's already too late," he said.

"That's right."

"What'll you do? You know who the father is?"

"I have a good idea who it is."

"It's not that easy to tell, is it?"

She shrugged.

"What a fix you're in."

"Right. But I can handle it somehow," she said, smiling her smile of goodness, ample lines creasing the face above the swollen torso.

He completely lost his desire to make love to her. Putting the flat of his hand on her abdomen, he slowly ran it down her curving belly. His hand descended, ending in a tufted lea; he then quickly withdrew his hand, stood up and put on his clothes. Handing money to her, her fee plus a little extra, he said his usual farewell—"Well, take care"—and left.

HE DIDN'T SEE HER after that. The other woman he frequented had moved out of the district, so he rarely set foot there. Shortly thereafter the quarter was legislated out of existence.[1]

---

1 Prostitution was outlawed in Japan in 1956.

Now, six years after he had gone into her room and run his hand over her distended belly, he was following her down a narrow alley. Walking through the slush, he recalled the past and wondered what she had been doing during those six years—and what he himself had been doing. There was only one thing he knew about himself: that he was now utterly exhausted. He was tormenting a woman and she was doing the same to him, a process that was proving to be endless. Or to put it another way, he continued to love a woman, and the woman continued to love him.

His companion's voice intruded into his thoughts.

"Is the live performance woman on woman or man on woman?"

His companion was talking to her. His tone was animated. You could tell he was enjoying the little adventure in the backstreets of the city.

Ah, I see this guy's senses haven't been dulled from too many sex films yet.

He remembered himself sitting in a small basement twelve years before. And he envied a bit the man walking next to him.

The woman stopped in front of an unassuming gate. Opening it, they found themselves before a frosted glass door, the back door of a small one-story house.

"Please wait here for a while," she said as she went into the house, leaving Kenji and the other man to wait in front of the glass door.

She showed the two men into a small room, then left. The room had no furniture or ornamentation whatsoever, just an expanse of frayed, jaundice-yellow tatami mats. The two men stood there and waited. Kenji was seized with the sensation that the moisture the tatami had absorbed was about to seep into his body through the soles of his feet.

"Looks like there's a visitor ahead of us," he muttered.

"I guess it means we wait until they're finished," his companion said, his tone jovial, then added cheerfully: "They're doin' it now!"

A muffled sound reverberated dully from the next room. It was a melancholy sound and loud enough to almost set the wall to shaking. It had a regular, rapid cadence. He saw in his mind's eye a resilient, soft mass being lifted up forcefully, then thrown down on the tatami with violent force— two fair, round, symmetrical globes of buttock flesh striking the tatami as if flung. In the next instant, rebounding up over the tatami, they once again descended full force.

The two men looked at each other silently.

The many live sex shows he had seen all followed a formula, much in the style of the exercise programs on morning radio. Thus the ferocious and passionate, or rather, the dismally ardent, sounds that came from the next room began to agitate his mind with curiosity and desire.

Suddenly the sliding paper door facing the hall opened and the woman who had brought them looked in.

"This way, please."

The two men went into the hall. The hall led past the next room and continued to the back of the house. The sound maintained its regular cadence.

The woman passed the next room ahead of the men and kept walking. The sliding door had been left open. The sound continued. As Kenji passed the open door he turned his head and glanced into the room. He did not see what he had expected to see.

A little girl was playing with a large rubber ball, bouncing it on the tatami. The ball, discolored to a dirty grey, went back and forth between the girl's small hand and the yellowed tatami at a fixed cadence. He stopped there in spite of himself. Sensing his presence, the girl held the ball in both hands and turned her face to him, a wisp of smile on her lips. It was an

— 21 —

innocent child's smile with no hint of gloom. Then she started bouncing her ball on the tatami again.

The woman ushered the men into a small room set off by itself at the back of the house. A fat young woman sat waiting there. There was a futon spread out in the center of the room.

"What's gonna happen with only one woman?" his companion said to himself. The woman who had led the men into the room smiled broadly and, without saying a word, began taking her clothes off.

His mind was once again dark and exhausted; he watched her angular shoulder bones appear from beneath her clothes. The bones he remembered from twelve years ago seemed to him even more obvious now.

On Houses

家屋について

Translated by Lawrence Rogers

I've moved around a lot all my life. Once when I was on a train trip I tried recalling all the houses I'd lived in.

Why did I attempt something like that? To say I did it just to kill time is the obvious answer, yet if you were to say that was not really the case, I wouldn't disagree.

The flow of time then had, unexpectedly, turned molasses-like. Time, which is normally transparent and flows on around me provoking no sense of resistance, now began to cling maliciously to me.

I expect everyone has experienced this. Ignored, time covers one like finely powdered glass.

It can also be like that when you're trying, to no avail, to get to sleep. Some have the idea that counting sheep works. As you're counting—one sheep, two sheep, three sheep—the bodies of the animals, covered with ash-colored ringlets, gradually pile up in your head and your mind's eye becomes choked with these ashen swirls, rendering you ready for sleep.

On a train in the bright light of day, however, I couldn't sleep. So to get through this burdensome time I decided to divert myself by thinking of the series of houses I'd lived in. And perhaps it is likewise not unprofitable to occasionally reflect on the life one has lived.

THE FIRST HOUSE I lived in was owned by my grandfather. The part that faced the street was his office. When you pushed open the heavy door of the office, a narrow concrete walkway extended straight back. If you went through the lattice door built partway down the walkway, you could see, further on, the main entrance to the residence.

The house was made up of three parts. Or rather, two two-storey buildings had been built in front of and behind a one-storey house, though with a good distance between them; the three sections were connected by the long walkway. This U-shaped walkway, which linked the several parts, was laid out so that it encompassed two courtyards. A single stone lantern stood in each of the courtyards.

The kitchen was large; the wooden floor area alone appeared to be eight mats in size, well over 100 square feet.

When you left either courtyard through a small gate, you saw a godown and a warehouse in the spacious garden, which extended to the residences.

Every time I recalled that house, connected as it was by the long walkway that ran ribbon-like far back into the grounds, I thought to myself, and not without nostalgia, what a curious layout it had.

Of course, my thinking it was the most curious of construc-tions started after I became aware of what normal houses looked like. It goes without saying that realization came to me after I had compared it with other homes.

As I rode the train I recalled in detail the layout of the com-pound. The roof of the single-storey section had a concrete veranda, and from here my grandfather would fly kites for me when I was a little boy. Recalling these details with a sense of the bittersweet, suddenly, quite suddenly, an idea about the house that I had never had before broke to the surface.

I'll bet Grandfather didn't build that house himself. He bought a restaurant and made it into a residence-cum-office, didn't he?

— 24 —

As this question presented itself to me I once again called to mind the layout of the house; it conformed splendidly with a plan for a Japanese-style restaurant: two courtyards and two stone lanterns, a kitchen with generous board flooring, the three isolated sections, each connected by the long walkway. And the place that he used as an office had most certainly been the restaurant's office.

Thus the house did not have a "curious layout"; when you consider that it was a real Japanese-style restaurant, it had nothing less than a supremely functional form.

This revelation briefly left me dumbfounded. The fact that I had not realized this until that moment on the train put me in an inexplicable frame of mind. I was dumbfounded not because the building I was born in had once been a restaurant, but because I had not realized that was the case.

Grandfather had about him the air of what you might call a moralist and was a hard-headed sort. He disinherited my father, who then left the house and moved to another city, taking his wife and children with him.

The residence that Grandfather lived in, however, was kept just as it had been built until it burned down in the air raids during the war. And by the time I became a college student I had returned to it many times and stayed there. And yet I had been unaware. Or rather, I was not even inclined to think about it.

Why was I not so inclined?

As I pondered this I discovered two things that could pass for reasons.

First, it was a given in my mind that because Grandfather worked as an architect it was only natural that he would have built the structure himself.

The second reason was due to my feeling that its curious layout played a functional role for the people who lived in it. Which is to say, three people—my grandfather, my grandmother (who did not get along with him and later moved out with my father), and my father, whose relationship with his father was such that he would later be disinherited—lived alone, each in his or her own part of the compound.

In other words, I vaguely comprehended that the layout of the house was not normal and was perhaps an aberration of a sort, doubtless because it was built, I reasoned, to meet the needs of these complicated human relationships.

I NOW RECALLED THE several parts of the residence with a fresh perspective.

Going outside through the kitchen entrance, you found a small brook. I remembered the feeling I had walking over the wooden bridge built over it. When the structure had been a restaurant surely patrons took pleasure in crossing the brook. As to why I should think this sort of thing, I have to say the sensation of walking on the bridge provoked in me a promiscuous frame of mind.[1]

When I returned to the house as a college student, I would quietly slip back into my room through the back door when coming back late at night because Grandfather was strict and did not approve of nocturnal amusements.

In fact, he was severity itself. Whenever he took me out we inevitably went into the hills on the outskirts of town. We would walk for a good while along the ridges of the hills that encircled the small city. He was near seventy years of age, but he was in robust health and his legs were stronger than mine. He was short, yet broad-shouldered, and had a moustache.

When I went out in the daytime by myself and went to see the touring tent theaters and the like, he would always have a question for me on my return.

"Where'd you go?"

"I've been walking in the hills," I would tell him.

And that would put him in good spirits.

---

[1] When prostitution was legal in Japan licensed districts were often surrounded by a moat and accessible by a footbridge.

And now on the train, when the several parts of the compound rose one by one to my consciousness, I at length recalled the interior of the storehouse, with its damp, musty, stale air, and one particular scene from the past.

My strict grandfather was rebuking a maid in front of the storehouse. The maid was an ill-favored young woman, extraordinarily fat, a puffed-up woman with a peachblow complexion. She was rough-hewn, but a good person.

I was a middle school student when I saw this. It was not unusual for Grandfather to chastise the servants. However, an uneasy feeling complicated this scene for me.

The maid was bawling loudly. And a measure of embarrassment underlay Grandfather's rebukes.

"Come now, you must stop your crying."

His tone was somewhat mollifying, and this made the maid wail only louder.

The instant I recalled this on the train almost twenty years after the fact, it immediately occurred to me that I understood the hidden meaning of the spectacle.

Hadn't Grandfather, almost seventy then, secretly been having an affair with the overweight, unattractive woman? I was sure of it.

Grandfather had his bedroom upstairs in a room in the two-storey building toward the front of the compound. And the maid's room was in a corner of the one-storey building. The heavy-set peachblow maid would make her way down the long walkway in the middle of the night, taking care to walk softly. Such a scene presented itself to me on the train. (Some time later I determined that what I had suspected had been the case.)

The recollection of this scene brought with it a dark—one might say painful—emotion.

When Grandfather lost his home in the air raid he took a room in a relative's house out in the countryside and kept very much to himself. I was in college then, and when I visited him I discovered he had grown a long grey beard and was beginning to show signs of decline. As he said goodbye he grumbled that he, too, was living in poverty now and pressed into my hand a small amount of money. This I also recalled with nostalgia and melancholy.

I HAD BEEN TWO years old when we left his house and moved to another city, so my recollections of the house grew out of the many visits I made later.

In our new city we had moved four times by the time I entered kindergarten. The configuration of these homes, however, is hazy in my memory. It would be fairer to say I have only fragmented memories of the lay of the neighborhoods.

We once lived in a house that stood at the top of a street. From there we could look out at a field rank with weeds. I can recall the sight of the setting sun dyeing the field crimson.

We also lived in a house built beside a stream. Over the stream lay a half-rotten log that served as a bridge to the other side. The path that ran alongside the stream went on and on, long, white, and dusty. I once walked a spell along that path when I was being taken to a photo studio to have my picture taken. I remember encountering a madman running amok, brandishing a long bamboo pole.

However, as I rode the train I now attempted to recall something with hidden meaning amongst the recollections entwined with those houses, rather than the shapes the houses took.

I had the feeling that a hidden meaning was right before me and would now certainly become as clear as day. And yet nothing of the sort happened.

I've lived in more than ten houses since the time I entered kindergarten. I could clearly recall the layout of these dwellings. I went on recalling, one after the other, simply how the houses looked.

All sorts of structures—big houses, small houses, newly-built houses, houses built in the Tokugawa era—rose to my consciousness, then disappeared.

We had also lived in a shack built on land so low-lying and wet one could well wonder if it was reclaimed swampland. I slept in a two-mat room by the earthen floor at the entrance, and when I woke my pillow had often fallen onto the dirt floor. The roof leaked, but the cramped space did not permit escape from the rain. I would sleep with an opened umbrella turned upside down, its curved handle hooked on the electric light cord. The fabric of the umbrella would hold water that leaked through the roof for quite a while.

One day a human being abruptly fell out of the sky and landed in front of the house, emitting animal-like groans as he writhed on the ground, a sound that seemed created by some machine. A lineman who had been up a telephone pole had been shocked and came crashing to the ground.

Why, I wondered, had only dismal recollections such as these presented themselves to me?

But I know why. As my reminiscences approached the house I last lived in, a melancholic shadow cast itself over me. I will doubtless reside in any number of houses as I live on, yet I will now tell you about what I'll call the last house I lived in. It's been about a year since I moved out of it, but it still stands deserted, just as it was when I left. It's a single-storey wood-frame house of only two rooms, with a rotting wisteria trellis that is about to collapse.

This is not to say that I cleared out of that place in order to move into a finer house; permit me here, however, to omit the particulars surrounding the move.

From time to time I stop by the house, which gives the impression of something groveling over the black earth. I said it's deserted, but I expect a single black cat is living there. The black cat was my pet. When I was leaving I picked it up and attempted to put it in the moving van. The cat, however, dug its claws into the back of my hand, leapt from the vehicle and ran into the house. I tried again and again to get it back into the van, but it was no use.

There's a saying: a dog attaches itself to its master, a cat to its house.

In the end I decided to leave the black cat in the house. I asked the neighbors if they would feed it, put a single cushion in the middle of the six-mat room and left.

I stop by and look inside, but I never see the animal.

"How is the cat doing?" I asked the neighbor.

"It never misses a meal."

"Where do you suppose it sleeps?"

"It seems to slip in through the sweep hole in the wall and sleep on the cushion."

I thanked him, unlocked the back door and went inside. The air had the damp smell of a vacant house, but I couldn't detect the odor of animal. Yet when I took a good look at the fabric of the cushion I had placed in the center of the room with its yellowed tatami, I could see plenty of fine grey animal hairs clinging to it.

I felt a shudder of emotion when I envisioned the black cat, in a half-crouch, slinking into the deserted house late at night, climbing onto the cushion, folding its legs under itself, and at last lying curled up into a compact ball.

MY REMINISCING ABOUT MY houses as I sat in my seat on a train running full throttle was at that point interrupted.

As I examined my emotion occasioned by the deserted house and my black cat, I attempted to uncover the meaning hidden behind it.

"It ought to be obvious by now," I mumbled to myself.

However, the shudder-like emotion that came to me seemed to have an extraordinarily complex shape. I was unable to comprehend the precise form it took.

ON HOUSES

And my frame of mind, which I had been able to divert by recalling the layout of the houses I had lived in, again began to reassert itself. Time came to adhere to a turbid whiteness and cling perversely to it. I concluded I would thoroughly and accurately examine as best I could this complicated form another day.

The Man Who Fired the Bath

風呂焚く男

TRANSLATED BY LAWRENCE ROGERS

The air inside the house stirred when he unlocked the front door and opened it. The smell of mold and dust filled his nostrils.

The house had been vacant the two months he had been away. He had not been traveling. He had been staying in one place and another around town, the same town the house was in. He had done such a tiresome, bootless thing because he had come to dread being in the house. He took off his shoes and was about to enter the next room when he looked behind himself. He sensed something, but the door was still shut. There was a thin film of dust on the flooring in the entryway and a straight line of footprints over it. These were his own footprints.

He hurriedly threw open the door to the verandah. His gaze fell on the small garden's black earth and the old fence. The fence was low, so he could see the side of his neighbor's house. The frosted glass door was still closed that day. Bright sunlight filled the room, highlighting two months of dust. Sallow, greenish mold was growing here and there on the tatami.

For a moment he stood in the middle of the small six-mat room and gazed at the expanse of mold and dust. Pushing aside a sense of sluggishness at last, he went to the kitchen, began filling a bucket with water, and threw in it a rag, rough and dried stiff as a sheet of tin. When he kicked off his socks the tatami matting felt powdery under his feet. He had the sensation he had crushed a moth underfoot wherever there was the sallow, greenish mold.

He went into the bath, removed the lid from the tub and turned on the water full force. He returned to the tatami room, grabbed the rag, got down on his hands and knees and began cleaning the tatami. When he had finished wiping it he returned to the bath, for he assumed the tub would be full. No water had collected in the tub, however. The powerful jet of water from the faucet dashed itself raucously against the wooden bottom of the tub in a spray of white.

He blinked at this, and for an instant his face was that of a little boy standing before a magician, his expression a mixture of fear, surprise and curiosity. He looked about the bath pointlessly. Again he sensed something unpleasant and his eye could not shake the image of the fluttering of the hem of a magician's black cape and the color red. This dark, yet garish, red was firmly lodged in a recess of his mind.

He knew what this unique color of red portended. Red terrified him.

He shook his head vigorously to dispel this apparition of a magician and the color red, bent over and looked down into the tub. The wood had dried out over two months, and cracks had opened between the boards. The bath water was running out through the cracks.

He suddenly felt mold and dust all over his body. It was still too early in the year to just douse himself with cold water. How could he plug up the cracks in the tub? A plasterer's mud, the putty glaziers use, these things, things akin to them, came to mind. He wondered if newspaper would turn into a soft mud or the like if he boiled it. He had a vague recollection to that effect, so he quickly made a pile in a washbasin out of newspapers that he had torn into small pieces, added water to it, and set it on the gas ring. The concoction in the washbasin did not at all turn out as he had anticipated. Irritated, he dumped the contents into the tub. This was not an act that had a clear purpose, but the paper that had begun to dissolve and the small scraps of paper on which he could still make out printing flowed into the cracks in the tub and were caught there, achieving the aim of filling the cracks, albeit only incompletely. In the end the tub filled up with water, though some still oozed out.

While the loss was slow, the water level was dropping perceptibly. He got in the tub, turning up the gas all the way, letting a small, steady stream of water into the bath. When he sank into the bath and closed his eyes, a sense of contentment—the water was at a delectable temperature—suffused his being. He opened his eyes and, still squatting in the hot water, raised his hands over his head and stretched, swaying his body back and forth several times. The bath water sloshed with the movement of his body, and the paper that had settled at the bottom of the tub rose to the surface. Fine white bits, foam-like and sticky, fragments of dissolved newsprint—these described a design on the surface of the bath. The pattern looked to him now to be a person's face. It was the face of a woman he knew. He instinctively stiffened his back and jerked his chin out of the bath water. A scrap of newspaper lazily floated up in front of his nose. He could see part of a headline from the metro page of the paper, a line of large print on a scrap that still held its shape: *Stabs to Death. . . .*

He stood up in the tub, moving like a mechanical doll. Bath water ran off the contours of his body; wet scraps of paper stuck to his skin. He quickly dried himself off and left the bath.

When he went back to the tatami room he set a stool against the wall and stood on it. He slid open the door to a small cupboard against the wall just below the ceiling. In it was a large bundle wrapped in a red cloth. It was a dark, yet insistent red. His hand, grasping the side of the bundle, abruptly splayed and pushed it further back.

He shut the door, made sure it was completely closed, then got down off the stool. Taking the stool away from the wall, he pushed it against the opposite wall. Ruminating briefly, he carried the stool to the kitchen. A desire to get as far away as possible from the wall with the cupboard gripped him.

Six months ago he had rented this house and moved in. He did so to live with Nobuko, and also to keep Akiko from knowing where he lived. However by the next evening this expectation had been betrayed. His doorbell had rung, and when he answered it there stood Akiko. He had no idea how she had found his new house, but there before him stood Akiko in the flesh. Nobuko had not yet moved in. Akiko stood there facing him, making no attempt to step into the entryway. She then turned on her heel and disappeared into the darkness. Not a word was exchanged between them; he would have to postpone Nobuko's move into the house.

From that day on Akiko rang the doorbell again and again. He realized that her visitations followed certain rules. For one thing, she never attempted to come into the house. She would stand on the concrete floor in the entryway and stare into his face, not saying a word. Sometimes her gaze traveled past him and focused on the wall behind him. When that happened, it seemed as though Akiko was trying to read with her whole being the atmosphere of the house. They would have a brief conversation.

"Don't come here anymore."

"Don't tell me that."

"Shall I move again?" He was muttering to himself.

"Won't do you any good to move."

Akiko's eyes seemed to be laughing. Then her retreating figure disappeared into the darkness.

The other thing was that Akiko never came after nine at night.

These two precepts for Akiko's visits, however, made him uneasy: they might fall away at some point. He had no guarantee that he would not awake one morning to find Akiko sitting silently by his bed. He had often considered moving. Yet when he thought of the immense amount of mental and physical effort that he would expend, in the end he stayed put in the house.

"Don't come here anymore."

"Don't tell me that."

Almost four months passed as this exchange was repeated again and again. Then one day their conversational routine changed.

"I may not come again," Akiko told him when she returned with a large bundle wrapped in red cloth that she had apparently first set down on the ground in front of the door. She picked it up and pressed it on him. His torso was obscured by the huge bundle.

"What's this?"

Akiko stared at him wordlessly, but no sooner had a faint smile slowly spread across her face than she was gone. And he was left with a large, dark, yet insistently red cloth-wrapped bundle in his house.

The entire contents of the large bundle were hand-sewn white underpants, a mound of white shorts, neatly folded along their creases and in two piles. He had lost no time in wrapping the stacks in the red cloth and putting it into the cupboard up near the ceiling so that it would not catch Nobuko's attention and he himself would be spared looking at it.

True to her word, from that day on Akiko never appeared at the house. From then on, however, fear began to gnaw at him. Akiko's visits had irked and angered him, and, true, they had bewildered him, but he had been able to maintain a strong posture resistant to fear.

Though he might make his stand, wholeheartedly throwing himself into the fray, his adversary was now stacks of white cloth. And yet inside the cupboard, tightly shut, the several dozen pairs of shorts had turned into a large, red living thing that lay biding its time as it considered the situation. In his mind's eye he clearly saw the faint rise and fall of the bundle's red shoulders, its breathing measured.

Nobuko's gaze would move toward the ceiling from time to time and fix itself on the cupboard door.

"What are you looking at?"

"I'm not looking at anything. Why do you ask?"

In that answer arose the form of the red bundle, breath bated in the dark cupboard, straining mightily to swell itself up and draw Nobuko's attention. When Nobuko was not home he would put the stool against the wall and, trying not to make a sound, climb up on it, then, stealthily putting his finger on the door, suddenly whip it open. Whenever he did that, however, the red bundle would return to being a simple object, now silent as stone. In the end, he had locked the front door and, together with Nobuko, left the house.

They had stayed at one and another inn around town; two months quickly passed. They did not stay long at any inn. That was because he sensed that Akiko might well turn up at their room in an inn and say, "If you two aren't going to be in the house with the red cloth bundle, I've no choice but to start visiting you again."

His finances would not permit them to continue their life in inns more than two months; expenses were mounting. This was the reason, more than any other, why he returned to the house.

HE PUSHED THE STOOL to a corner of the kitchen and surveyed the room, now minus its dust and mildew. When he recalled the red bundle lurking inside the cupboard against the wall, however, his gloom was little changed from before the house-cleaning.

He went out onto the verandah and looked at the yard. A spindly tree had been planted by the low fence, an old fence, and its slender branches had new, light green leaves. The leaves, absolutely still, were translucent in the light of the sun.

No breeze today, I'd say.

He looked about the tiny yard, his eyes considering its size. He was wondering if there was enough room in the yard for a bonfire. He was wondering if he would be able to burn several dozen pairs of shorts. Which meant that his fear of those articles had lessened somewhat over two months. Before, once he had shut it away in the cupboard, the red bundle had begun from that very moment on to come to life in the darkness, and the countless stitches of the several dozen pairs of shorts had been transformed into countless sharp needle points which jutted up at the skin on his hands. Which was why he had had not the slightest inclination to open the cupboard door and grab hold of the bundle.

The yard before him seemed, after all, too small to have a bonfire.

Out of the blue he heard a man's voice, loud and rasping.

"Hi. You've been away for some time, haven't you?"

The glass door of the house next door, which had earlier been shut, was now wide open and a middle-aged man stood on his verandah. The two men faced each other over the low fence. The neighbor, a stocky man with a brawny build, had a genial expression on his face. When he had run into him on the street from time to time he had stopped and chatted. There was no reason to believe the man hadn't noticed his chaotic lifestyle, yet his neighbor never acted as though he had. It may have been his imagination, but sometimes he thought he saw a sharpness in the eyes of the genial, smiling face.

"Did you take a trip somewhere?"

He heard no malice in the other man's tone, yet he felt as though he was being sounded out. He then tried changing the thrust of the conversation somewhat.

"Yes . . . well . . . but when you are away a good while you have to leave your tub full of water, don't you."

"Water?"

"My tub got bone dry, cracks developed, and it started leaking."

"Oh, that's what you're talking about! Then there's no problem. You just dump a bag of rice bran into the tub and it'll plug it up for you right then and there."

"Rice bran?"

He reflexively repeated the words; he was surprised that his neighbor, with his brawny build and deeply sunburned skin, would have such knowledge.

"Right. Rice bran you get at the rice dealer."

He queried him again: "Is that right? I am surprised you know something like that. It's not the sort of thing you would expect a man to know. I took newspaper and . . ."

He began to explain, then stopped himself. For he saw himself in his mind's eye as he set the washbasin on the gas burner and boiled down the newsprint: a pathetic, ludicrous figure. He changed the subject.

"I'd been thinking of applying cement inside the tub."

"I've a bit of worthless knowledge myself. I've been through the mill, you know."

His neighbor laughed, his white teeth flashing, but the rare hint of a wry smile passed across the unremarkable expression on the man's face. That hint seemed to him to suggest that his neighbor had detected the chaos of his private life. Flustered, he decided to end the conversation.

"Is that right? Well then, I'll have to try it right away."

He started to go back into the house. His neighbor's voice pursued him.

"Ah, and in your house . . ."

He stopped and looked back.

"You don't have any cockroaches?"

"Well, I haven't noticed any yet."

"If you see signs of them, please give me a holler. I'll show you how to eliminate them."

Only kindheartedness seemed to show itself in the man's face, yet he felt as though he was being mocked.

He again looked into the bath. The wooden tub had lost two-thirds of its water. Nonetheless, he could not bring himself to follow his neighbor's instructions and toss a packet of rice bran into the tub.

"If I'm not going to use rice bran. . . ."

Should he coat the inside of the tub or ought he get rid of it? While these two ideas—or rather, entities more akin to emotions—intermingled in his mind, a plan suddenly came to him. He would remodel the bath, then get an old-fashioned Goemon tub.[1] He would get rid of the wooden tub and replace it with the heavy iron cauldron-like tub. An iron tub would never develop cracks. And he would apply cement around it to set it in place.

Going ahead with the plan would take most of his savings, and he could expect that finding a dealer to install an old-style Goemon tub would not be easy. But he didn't think twice about it. To the contrary, the plan captivated him.

A Goemon stokehole was reborn in his memory. The rectangular opening, utterly flame-colored, flickered violently, a mix of crimson and orange, and roared a fire's roar.

As long as it is something that will burn, the rectangular opening will set aflame any and everything and consume it utterly. Even insect carcasses, dried fruit peelings, and, of course, shorts made of cloth. His desire for the flaming stokehole was as petulant as that of a thirsty man wanting water. He hurriedly locked the door and left the house.

THE REMODELING OF THE bath took three days. When the metal tub, unpainted, arrived on the bed of a small truck, it looked to him like a gigantic lump of iron.

---

1 An old-style metal bathtub, usually cast iron, in which the water is heated by a wood-fed flame under the vessel. Named after the legendary sixteenth century brigand Ishikawa Goemon, who was put to death by boiling in oil.

"What in the world were you thinking—giving up a gas *furo* and bringing in an old-fashioned tub like that?"

The tone of the prosecutor was in Nobuko's voice.

She called it an old-fashioned tub, and it certainly didn't look as though it should be on the bed of a modern truck. It would have been appropriate if it had been transported on a large horse cart and tied down with straw rope. Yet if a Goemon tub secured with straw rope had arrived, cart creaking away, given the state of his nerves he might well have taken the tub for a suspicious-looking intruder. Even when the small truck brought the tub in a completely matter-of-fact fashion, the sound of its undeniably perky engine reverberated loudly, and provoked in him an emotion very much like fear.

Sunlight fell on the tub and cast a gigantic shadow on the ground, at which point he had a premonition of misfortune.

He didn't respond to Nobuko immediately, then said, "I'll grant you it's old-fashioned."

"What in the world were you thinking?" Nobuko asked again in exasperation.

"Well, it's a whim."

"You can't just say it's a whim and let it go at that!"

The workers set the tub on the ground with a heavy thud. Nobuko knitted her brows like someone who had suffered an affront. Her tone told him she had no doubt at all that he was up to something. And, in fact, he *was* up to something. He intended to shove several dozen pairs of shorts through the fire door and reduce them to ashes.

He had to carry out his scheme before Nobuko could get wind of it. When he first met Nobuko she was naturally not familiar with his clothes. They were things that he himself had picked out, that he himself had bought, or that Akiko had bought for him.

At first Nobuko was restrained and had given him small presents she had bought and had wrapped, gifts of socks or neckties. He casually accepted these as signs of goodwill. If

Akiko questioned him about something he would simply say he saw it in a display window in town and that would be the end of the matter.

Suddenly, however, Nobuko sent him a present that couldn't be ignored. It was a suit, and it clung to his body like his own skin, which was her intent. If he had not been in love with Nobuko it would not have presented any problem. All he need have done was store it in a corner of the closet. He imagined Akiko's eyes riveting themselves on the suit; this troubled him and engendered some guilt. A certain amount of annoyance was also in the mix of feelings.

He assayed an imaginary conversation with Nobuko.

"You needn't hurry things along so."

"How's that? I don't know what you're talking about."

"My suit looks to you the same as my skin, right? Listen, I'm saying that you ought not try to hurry changing my skin into a skin that no one else touches."

"Dear me, I never even thought such a thing. I came across material that I thought would look so very good on you that I just forgot myself and bought it."

"I'm delighted you feel that way, but you can be sure the emotion I'm talking about has entered your heart without your being aware of it."

Nobuko says nothing. Her look of denial is quite apparent. For women, that which writhes in the world beneath consciousness is as good as non-existent. For a woman, that is always the case, so what is one to say of that creature we know as woman? Considering the subconscious as non-existent leads to confusion in the conversation between men and women, conversation attempting to resolve one question, and one that becomes pinned within narrow confines and loses its vitality. Quite suddenly his temper flares and he begins shouting.

"Don't try to control me like that!"

Nobuko reflexively shouts back at him. It seems to him she has been waiting for her cue.

"There's no way I'm controlling you! All I did was buy it out of affection for you. And then you look at it in such a twisted, self-centered way."

He had exhausted himself continuing his imaginary conversation to that point. In the end, the spite he felt toward Nobuko, his partner in conversation, came to be directed at women in general and all that remained for Nobuko was affection.

This emotion impelled him; time passed and he was able to serenely wear both the new suit and a new raincoat around Nobuko.

He hoped that she would see the change in their relationship and the significance of their connection, gradually becoming more apparent as the days went by and that this would register with her, yet Nobuko rushed things all the more.

If he happened to be wearing socks that he had discovered in a display window in town, socks whose design had caught his fancy, her expression would harden.

"Where'd you get those?"

"Hey, I bought them."

Nobuko would wordlessly open a drawer, take out a pair of socks of her own choosing, and set about taking off the socks he had on. As she removed them he wondered if she might well tear the skin right off his feet.

He could not let Nobuko notice the existence of the red bundle with its several dozen pairs of shorts. And he could not let her see him shoving it through the bath's stokehole. If she were not to accept his explanation for his old-fashioned remodeling of the bath as a whim, he had to come up with a justification for it.

"The fact is, these days I'm terribly irritable. When I was like that as a student, I'd fire up a Goemon tub and that would calm me down. It seems to be good for my nerves to toss kindling through a stokehole piece by piece as I gaze at the flames. I simply remembered that."

Nodding, Nobuko did not press him, yet the look on her face did not suggest that she was persuaded.

HE WAS SURE HE would be able to live with Nobuko after the red bundle had been burned.

"You can move in once the bath's been remodeled," he had told Nobuko. "The place will be a mess until then."

So it was that he had to quickly destroy the red bundle. He waited for a time when Nobuko would not be there. The day came when she had business to attend to all day and could not be expected to drop by. He put kindling through the stokehole, and when it was burning nicely he brought in the red bundle.

He had been impatiently waiting for this moment, yet when he slipped the hand-sewn white shorts into the fire one by one he was hesitant and began having second thoughts. He felt a faint pain on the skin of his hands. He vividly recalled the moment he shut the red bundle up in the darkness of the cupboard and it became a living thing.

Each time he slipped a pair of shorts through the stokehole—the fire was now a roaring meld of crimson and orange—he suspected it might get damper and damper inside until finally water puddled and put out the flames. He fell victim to this intense misgiving, yet the fire continued to burn fiercely.

When he had finished burning all the cloth—there could well have been fifty pairs—his fatigue weighed heavily on him and his mind was a blank.

"Oh, you're heating the water for the bath, are you?"

He heard Nobuko's voice behind him. Instinctively he looked at the ground in front of the stokehole, but there was no indication that the red bundle had been there.

"Hey, I thought you weren't able to come by today!"

"Well, I was able to."

Nobuko laughed softly as she spoke, but there was suddenly a suggestion of more than a little doubt in her face; her eyes went to the area around the stokehole.

"Maybe I'll take a bath myself later."

"You needn't wait until later. I'm not bathing today."

"Wait, if you're not getting in, why heat up the water?"

"Well, I intended to when I started to heat the water, then, you know, I got tired. It's weird."

"If you're tired the bath'll refresh you."

"Yeah, but right now it's too much trouble. I'll get in a little later."

"Really? Okay, then I'll bathe."

He soon heard the sound of water coming from the bath. The hot bath water in the tub enveloped every inch of Nobuko's body and was infused with the scent of her skin. It was, in fact, the warmth of her skin that permeated the bath water. He would see this in his mind's eye whenever he listened to her bathing, but today was different. Each molecule of hot water bonded with her every cell and its heat permeated each. The heat generated by the burning of several dozen hand-sewn pairs of shorts had suffused her being.

Nobuko emerged from the bath, an ambiguous expression on her face. She took the futon out of the closet and crept under the quilt.

"What's the matter?"

"I don't know why, but I don't feel so good."

He had a sense of foreboding, but the urge to reject it was the stronger. And yet no sooner had he realized that a patch of skin on Nobuko's chest had turned into a little hillock, red and swollen, than the patch grew before his eyes, her whole body turning red and swollen. He touched her skin; she was burning up.

"I wonder if it's hives. I'll bet the fish I had for lunch was bad."

He said nothing.

"Go get me some medicine."

When he went outside and set off on his errand, his next-door neighbor was standing at his own front gate. He appeared to be gazing up at the sky, crimson from the setting sun.

"Hi, haven't seen you for a while," the man said, calling out to him. "By the way, how was the rice bran?"

The bath was on the opposite side of the house, away from his neighbor, but he guessed that the people coming and going during the remodeling had caught his neighbor's attention. He looked at the man's face and wondered if he really had not noticed the commotion. The expression on the man's face, however, was genial.

"The fact is I had a new tub installed, a Goemon tub. Well, of course I'm quite familiar with the effectiveness of rice bran. I'd been thinking of using it for some time."

The tone of his response was defensive; the other man's remained normal.

"Is that so? That's excellent! A Goemon will warm you to the core. To the core."

He looked at the man's face in spite of himself. All he saw was the genial expression.

He bought the medicine and returned home. He stopped in front of the tub's stokehole. The idea came to him to open it and look inside, for he suspected that there, still unburned—no, impervious to flame—he would find a dark, ponderous mass asprawl amongst the ashes.

He bent down, his face close to the stokehole. But then he straightened up and walked into the house, the small fire door unopened.

Perfume Bottles

香水瓶

TRANSLATED BY HIROKO IGARASHI AND LAWRENCE ROGERS

I ONCE WAS THINKING of writing about a prostitute who had abandoned her calling. I was going to make the central character a woman who had gone from the so-called red light district to the world outside, the setting historical, when the so-called red light districts had not yet been abolished. But when she is at last able to go outside, the pull on her of her former venue would begin to assert itself little by little. The outside world would attempt to sniff out her former life, to expose it and to push her back into it. (It's not that such forces are not at work, but they're not decisive.)

The strongest force lies inside herself, and it is slowly but surely driving her back into her past life. That life looks abnormal to those on the outside, but for her it becomes what you could call her daily life. Throughout that daily life the things that seep into the very cells of her body work upon her with a power that overwhelms reason. Thus she is gradually being drawn back to her previous station. I wanted to write about its persistence and the fear it held for her.

I wanted to gather concrete substantiation for the topic. What did I do to get this? In a part of my short story "The Tale of an Octopus" I touched on this. I've partially quoted that part here.[1]

---

1 The half-dozen paragraphs that follow also appear, with little change, as the conclu-

A CERTAIN DAY. I went down the stairs leading to the basement of a building. I'd heard a rumor that a prostitute I'd frequented some years before was working at a coffee shop in the basement. And I missed her. I was concerned about how she was working out there. At the same time I had my ulterior motive: material for a story.

She was sitting at the cash register. I hadn't expected it, but she looked at ease on the job. We agreed to get together after she got off work.

After a half an hour or so we were sitting face-to-face at another coffee shop and chatting.

The expression on her face suggested she had missed me too. The atmosphere was relaxed. As we were chatting away I slipped in my question. Her face tensed abruptly and she now sat rigid in her chair.

"You can't get any material for your stories from me anymore," she said, her words now measured and formal.

One night several months later I was again going down the steps to the coffee shop. There was a situation I absolutely had to ask her about. I needed it for a piece of fiction I was writing then. In the right-hand pocket of my jacket was a bottle of imported perfume and in the left a woman's cigarette lighter. I touched them from the outside of my pockets as I descended the stairs. To give these things to her might well insult her, perhaps make her even angrier than she had been before. This anxiety notwithstanding, I walked down the stairs slowly, fully intending to hand them to her.

And what do you think her response was when I gave her those two items?

Her delight was unaffected.

"You remembered the perfume I use, didn't you!"

I was flummoxed. I had given her the perfume Tabu. I knew next to nothing about perfume, and had not given any thought

sion to the short story "Tako no hanashi" (The Tale of an Octopus). See *Yoshiyuki Junnosuke zenshū*, vol. 5, Kōdansha, 1983, pp. 120–121.

to what she might use. I guessed that Tabu meant something like "forbidden" in Japanese. You could say that at the perfume counter the name had worked its will on me in my near-ignorance and had me pick it out.

I decided to answer her honestly.

"Actually, I didn't know what you liked. The purchase was pure guesswork."

My answer, however, did not bring a hint of disappointment to her face.

"But this is just what I wanted. I was running out of perfume and thinking I should buy more."

There was no particular reason for me to choose perfume and a lighter as presents. I chose them because they were neither large nor bulky and, considering my income, pretty luxurious. In this conversation, however, the focus was on the perfume. The word "forbidden" had taken firm hold of my emotions.

I now hesitated. What I wanted to ask her she could well see as indeed forbidden. I did not want my question to turn my cherished presents into contaminated merchandise that came with an ulterior motive.

Nonetheless, this was one year after the red light districts had been abolished. Nothing could again force her back to where she had been. Still, I couldn't ask my question and instead said, "How about a drink after you finish work?" She nodded.

I decided to spend the thirty minutes or so until the coffee shop closed in a bookstore in town. I looked at the spines of the books lined up on the shelves, and occasionally picked out one and examined the contents.

I soon found the title *Nursery Rhymes of the World* on the spine of a book on a shelf in the corner.

"I didn't know this had come out again," I mumbled, taking the book and skimming through it. I had the same book on my own bookshelf. I'd found mine in a used bookstore. Several short stories of mine were inspired by nursery rhymes in it.

I nostalgically flipped through the pages and checked the contents. I found that they were not entirely identical with my copy. A nursery rhyme caught my eye. It was entitled "The Devil."

In the morning when ye rise
Wash your hands, and cleanse your eyes.
Next be sure ye have a care
To disperse the water farre.
For as farre as that doth light,
So farre keepes the evill Spright.[2]

She herself was manifest in this nursery rhyme. In the outside world she wakes up in the morning and washes her face. In modern times, when we have a sink beneath the faucet, a well and a basin filled with water exist simply as metaphor, but nonetheless, the devil itself is hiding in the water she has washed her face in. The memory of her longtime day-to-day habits in the red-light district shakes and agitates her cells and appeals to her soul.

She holds the basin with water in front of her and goes a good distance to dump it. She goes to throw the water away so she'll not have to see it. Or she slowly pours it into the drain to keep it from spilling. Perhaps she needs this kind of circumspection.

"Of course, I can't ask her," I muttered to myself, closing the book and pushing it back in place.

AN HOUR LATER I was sitting face to face with her in a private tatami room in a small Japanese-style restaurant. Intoxication gave a faint rosy cast around her eyes. I was also beginning to feel the alcohol deep inside me.

2 This version of the Robert Herrick (1591–1674) poem is taken from *The Complete Poetry of Robert Herrick*, J. Max Patrick, editor, New York University Press, 1963, p. 426.

"Kuroda's okay, is he?" I asked, venturing her patron's name. The middle-aged man I hadn't yet met was as kind to her as ever. It was Kuroda who brought her to the world outside and placed her in her present situation. That she was sitting at the cash register meant that she had been given the responsibility of the coffee shop.

"He's fine, as always."

"And you're okay now, are you?" I asked. "You've settled down, right?"

Kuroda had got her out of the district twice, and twice she had gone back. This was the third time.

She smiled and said nothing. That she forced a smile and averted her eyes was out of shyness.

"Even if there's a problem, there's no place you can return to now," I told her.

She said nothing.

"But when I think of the places that have disappeared, you know, I feel nostalgic for them. But that may be a man's selfish ego speaking."

Suddenly I sensed the warmth of her skin. Wrapped in a kimono, she was, in my mind, stripped naked; I could sense her warmth as if it were my own. She was sitting on the other side of a low dining table placed on the tatami. I had spent a lot of time in her room when she was in the district. It was in fits and starts, but when you added it up it was a considerable amount of time. The memory of those days suffused my body.

I felt her eyes probing my face. Soon I would stand up, go around to her side of the table, and take her shoulders in my hands. I sensed there was no point in remaining seated, and began shifting strength to my knees and calves folded under me. The instant I became aware of what I was doing she stood up.

It was obvious she rose because she read my intentions. If I had stood she certainly would have moved to avoid me, but I was still sitting. She was momentarily confused; she moved toward the window as if carried by the wind and rested her gaze on the view outside.

I stood up, drew closer, then hesitated behind her.

"You can see a lot of neon signs, can't you," she said, making little effort to avoid me.

These were meaningless words that needed no answer. I put my hands on her shoulders. She violently twisted away from me,

"Don't do that!" she said, her voice harsh, almost a scream.

"Why not?"

She said nothing.

"You haven't cheated on him even once since you started working at the coffee shop?" I asked, wanting to make sure.

"Not once."

"Why not?"

"'Cause it would be all downhill after that."

I said nothing.

"Make it easy for me," she said.

I gently let my hands fall from her shoulders. I remembered the lines from the nursery rhyme: *For as farre as that doth light, / So farre keepes the evill Spright.*

It was then that I completely abandoned the idea of asking the question I had at the ready.

ONE NIGHT A YEAR later I put a perfume bottle in my pocket and went down the steps to the coffee shop.

"Your timing is good," she said. "I was about to run out of it and thinking I'd soon have to buy a new bottle."

I waited for her to finish work. We drank together, exchanging innocuous gossip, then went our separate ways.

Another year passed; I met her, perfume bottle in my pocket.

"It takes me exactly one year to use up this perfume. I was thinking it's time for you to show up 'cause the perfume's about gone."

We spent our time together as we had the previous year. Yet another year passed.

"We meet once a year, don't we," she said as she took the bottle of perfume.

"I go down the stairs thinking that you might no longer be there."

"I'll always be there."

"I'm impressed. With you, of course, but also with Kuroda."

"Well," she paused. "He *is* pretty calculating."

Her tone was like the wife who casually bad-mouths her husband. At the same time I could also sense in her words the pride of a woman who for a long time was the main draw at a first-class brothel in the red-light district. And her words also held criticism for me: it wasn't as though she alone was benefitting, nor did she want the praise one might give a social worker.

Yet another year passed.

"It's good to also have a friend you simply chat with like this," she said, watching my face and gauging my reaction. "Are you still up to your old tricks?"

"Well, sort of."

"I'm surprised it doesn't bore you," she said.

"You mean you've more than had your fill of it?"

"Uh-huh." She stared off into space. It was apparent she was now recalling her life as it had been before. Although I expected she would soon dispatch those memories, she continued to stare off into space.

"You've had your fill of it, have you?" I asked again. She looked at me with the eyes of someone just awakened.

"Well, I guess, kind of," she said. "Have you ever gotten a blood test?" She asked as though the idea had just come to her.

"Blood test? You mean to determine blood type?"

"No, not that kind."

"A test for syphilis?"

"Yes."

I looked at her face with fresh eyes. That kind of subject had never come up for discussion during these five years. Matters that reminded her of her previous life were avoided utterly; they were dangerous. What had happened to her?

"I got examined about six months ago," I told her. "I get that test from time to time, just to be safe."

"And?"

"It was negative. I got three different kinds of tests, and all the results were negative."

"Well," she said, "that's good."

"It is?"

"Mine was positive. I was sure I'd been cured, but a year ago I tested positive. This time I got honest-to-God treatment, and I'm completely cured now."

Her tone was surprisingly matter-of-fact.

"One day when I put my hands on your shoulders," I ventured with a smile, "you refused me and asked me to make it easy for you. Remember? But if something insinuates itself into your body, you can't refuse it."

"Refuse?"

"I mean it reminds you, willy-nilly, of what you were doing those days."

"Right. I was totally carried back. But I didn't recall it that vividly."

"I see. It was as if you were looking at some postcards you'd collected when you were a kid, maybe."

"Right. When the treatment was over, it all appeared to be postcards to me. Because a long time had already gone by, hadn't it."

If her life in the red light district seemed to her to be no more than scenes from old postcards. . . .

I asked myself if I should ask my question, but I now realized I was no longer interested in asking it. I took out a deep olive-colored perfume bottle, having made sure the name could be translated into Japanese as "forbidden."

"How about trying a different perfume next year?" I suggested.

The Illusionist

手品師

Translated by Lawrence Rogers

Kurata was taking a leisurely walk along a street he was unfamiliar with. He was thirsty and decided as he walked along that he'd like to have a beer. The doors of the bars that caught his eye from time to time on both sides of the street were shut tight. It occurred to him that most of the bars had small entranceways that faced the street, and there were doors of all sorts in those entranceways. That was as it should be, of course, and there was no need for him to feel that he was being rejected.

Nonetheless, he did not feel he could jauntily push open the door of an establishment he had never seen before. He felt a sense of strangeness. He had heard this was an area that had its share of dangerous bars.

The door of a bar he was looking at that very moment opened. A young man wearing wooden sandals with straw insoles came through the doorway, followed by a young woman with a fair complexion. Her skin was clear and she wore essentially no makeup; her physique was still that of a young woman.

"Well, I'll be back, okay?" the man said, briefly turning to face her and giving a vigorous wave goodbye. He then quickly turned away from her and began walking. The girl worked at the bar. The smile on her lips was obviously purely commercial, but it remained even after the man was well on his way. She was not smiling out of a warm feeling for the patron. Rather, Kurata sensed she was not used to suddenly turning off her smile.

Kurata found this agreeable and, at the same time, a source of relief. He reasoned that if the bar had such a woman it probably could not be a dangerous place.

The girl stood with her back to the door, the smile still on her lips. It was as though she was reluctant to go back into the bar with that expression on her face. Kurata was standing in front of her.

"You work here, right?"

"Yes."

"I can go in, can I?"

The girl, her expression earnestness itself, moved out of his way and motioned him to pass by.

"You go first," he said, those few words couched in friendliness.

He was sitting on a bar stool drinking a beer when he heard a man's voice at his ear.

"Mr. Kurata . . . You're Kurata Tatsuo, aren't you?" He turned his head and was confronted by a boy's face, its eyes staring hard in seeming challenge. The speaker was small and had a child-like face; Kurata immediately assumed he was a boy, but he was drinking in a bar, so he was doubtless a young man. Kurata wrote fiction. From time to time his photo did appear in newspapers and magazines, but his face was not well known. So this young man who spoke to him, a man he'd never seen before, was apparently a youth who was interested in literature. He decided the challenge in the eyes was without malice and probably came from the excitement of speaking to him, yet Kurata was annoyed. He was not fond of talking about literature when he was drinking.

"Do you come here often?" the young man asked.

"No, tonight's the first time. I was passing by and just thought I'd come in and check it out."

"For a change of pace?"

"Well, yes."

Kurata had been writing, secluded in a room in a small hotel in a district some twenty minutes away by car. The work had been difficult and tiring, so he had slipped out of the room and set off to look at the river. He had stood on a bridge and gazed at the water. It was a dark river that flowed through the city's flatlands and over which wafted a foul odor. And yet the lights of the city reflected on the surface of the stagnant river were beautiful, and his sinuses finally inured themselves to the smell, and the evening breeze was pleasant.

"My name is Kawai," the young man said, introducing himself. He lived near Kurata's hotel. "Are you writing in the hotel now?"

"That's right. Why do you ask?"

"Something to that effect appeared in a gossip piece."

Kurata's annoyance deepened. There was a growing and conspicuous number of young people who formed an image of a writer in their minds having read only gossip about him but not a single literary work by the author. Draining his glass of beer, he said nothing. He decided it was the right time to leave. The youth who called himself Kawai spoke again.

"I have loved reading your work for some time. I have read a good many other authors, but yours are curiously attuned to my psychology. I can completely relate to even the slightest detail in your work."

Kawai mentioned one of the author's stories as an example and began talking about a particular passage in it. It was clear he was not lying about being a fan of Kurata's writing, but the youth's eagerness annoyed him.

"You've read my work?" Kurata said, getting ready to leave. "I'd say that's commendable."

Kawai spoke rapidly now.

"I wonder if I might visit you at your hotel."

His language and attitude was quite proper. This idea was, nonetheless, unwelcome.

"Listen, it's where I'm doing my work, so . . ."

"Oh, I won't bother you while you're working. I'll provide a change of pace when you tire."

Kurata was in a bad mood now.

"But talking about literature when I'm working merely exhausts me mentally that much faster."

"I wouldn't visit you to talk about literature. I'd like to show you some magic."

"Magic?"

"And I'll show you how it's done."

Kurata looked at the other's face. He was not particularly curious about magic itself; his interest lay in the men who practiced it. Kawai, looking for support, turned to the girl standing on the other side of the bar.

"Yes, Kawai's magic is not at all amateurish."

She spoke to Kurata, her eyes staying on Kawai. Her expression was a bit too earnest, and for an instant her eyes—only her eyes—smiled. Kurata took his measure of Kawai and the girl.

"I guess you come here a lot, eh?"

"Now and again," the girl said, answering for Kawai. There was a moment of silence, then Kawai spoke.

"I'd like to come everyday, if I could."

"Are you a student?"

If he were, a high school uniform would suit him best. He had yet to lose his boyish looks.

"No, I work. At a company that makes furniture."

"I see."

Kurata looked casually around the bar. It was a cheap place; the only seats were the stools at the bar. A few drinks probably wouldn't cost that much. For Kawai, however, the tab would probably be a burden. This thought vaguely came to Kurata as he looked about the room. The interior had apparently been done in a northern European style, but at the end of a shelf full of Western liquor bottles sat a red Daruma doll.

"That your doll?" Kurata asked the girl.

"It belongs to the proprietress."

Kurata looked at the one blank eye and the eye which had been painted in with India ink.

"What do you suppose she's wishing for?"[1]

"That I don't know."

The girl smiled and Kawai, irritated, broke into the conversation.

"*Sensei*," he said, then immediately caught himself. "Mr. Kurata, might I visit you?"

"That'll be fine."

"When would be good?"

"Day after tomorrow. Let's see, how about coming by after work?"

THAT DAY KURATA SAT facing Kawai in a corner of the hotel lobby. There was a small table between their two chairs. Kurata wasted no time in restricting the scope of the discussion.

"How long have you been doing magic?"

"It's been about ten years. I've a friend I did it with, and he's now a professional magician."

"Ten years? Then I guess you must be pretty good," Kurata said, leaning all the way back in his chair and encouraging the youth. "Now, can you show me something?"

There were a lot of people in the lobby, all engaged in their own quiet conversations. The fact that magic was about to begin in one corner was for Kurata a source of roguish amusement.

When Kawai undid his cloth bundle, fingers deliberate, he exposed an ancient rectangular cardboard box. Kurata could tell from the writing on the outside of the box that it had once

---

1 The custom is to paint in the second eye after one's wish has been realized.

contained a transistor radio. When Kawai opened the lid, the writer saw a well-arranged complement of soiled playing cards, small red balls, and a turquoise handkerchief of sheer silk.

From the bottom of the box Kawai gingerly pulled out a black cloth and with even greater care opened it up on the table. It was a black velvet cloth edged in gold lace, the cloth a stage magician uses atop a small table that he puts his props on. But because the cloth was much smaller than the real thing, it couldn't cover the entire table. It lay flat at the center of the table, leaving the rest of it bare. The gold lace had turned rust red. The velvet on the cloth itself was worn and here and there was threadbare and grey. Kawai smoothed out the cloth with his palm, gently, with affection.

Kurata smiled. No matter how it might appear in the doubting eyes of the people in the lobby, it was obvious from Kurata's posture that his anticipation was real. Feeling protective of the young man, his focus on the movements of Kawai's fingers was intense.

The magic that Kawai was performing was run-of-the-mill, but done with a practiced, adept technique. He showed his palms and the backs of his hands: he held nothing. With a flutter of his hand a single red ball was suddenly wedged between two fingers. The number of balls grew, wedged, in the end, between all his fingers.

As Kurata watched the modest magic he remembered a story about a particular poet. The man, an excellent poet, was entangled in troublesome personal relationships, and as a result his wife left him and he spent his declining years alone. He had a child, a daughter. One night when she happened to look into the library upstairs she saw the poet sitting at his desk continuously moving his fingers, practicing with red finger balls.

When Kurata heard this story, the man's sense of isolation profoundly moved him as if it were his own. Yet the face of the young man he saw before him clearly retained the look of youth, shining with delight and triumph.

Moments later, however, Kurata noticed something. He caught sight of Kawai's fingertips as he began to lay out the cards on the black velvet cloth. The nails of his fingers were all cut deeply back. But they had not been trimmed with scissors; they had jagged edges, as though they had been chewed. Bitten back deeply, the chewing didn't stop at the tips of the fingernails; it reached into the fleshy round tips of the fingers.

"Uh-oh," Kurata said without thinking, "what happened to your fingers?"

He sensed agitation in the youth.

"I suppose you have to cut the nail to the quick to do magic."

Kurata had said that more to gloss over the youth's unease, but in an instant Kawai had hidden his fingertips in clenched fists.

"No, that's not the case," he replied shyly.

Kurata now saw another side of Kawai, one of melancholy isolation behind his outwardly cheerful facial expression. He would bite his nails when he was by himself, and gradually more irritated, chew them off, behavior he was no longer able to stop, like a ball rolling downhill. Ten fingers dyed red by oozing blood. The fleshy round tips of the fingers glistened with a bizarre sheen.

Kawai quickly began moving his fingers, performing a card trick. It was one that Kurata had seen more than once, but he watched eagerly.

"Excellent! I suppose in the end it's the practice you've done with the fingertips that counts, isn't it."

"That's right. In the beginning I would wake up and realize I'd been moving my fingers in my sleep. I've also had my finger muscles ache and swell up."

"It's tough to really master something, no matter what it might be. And it took you ten years, did it?"

"Ten years," Kawai said, his expression that of one savoring the passage of ten years' time.

"By the way, did you see how I did it?"

"Haven't a clue."

"This is how it's done."

Kawai once again laid cards on the black cloth and showed Kurata the secret to the trick. He then moved on to the next magic trick.

"Haven't a clue," Kurata said again, wanting to encourage the young man. Something occurred to him out of the blue.

"It must get to you when someone figures out your trick."

"That's true, but even if they really *don't* get it, you get discouraged, I'll tell you."

Kurata looked at Kawai once again and smiled wryly.

Two days later he got a phone call from Kawai in his hotel room. The young man was in high spirits.

"Ikuta Tenkon is giving a performance," he said, mentioning the name of a famous young magician. "Shall I get a ticket for you?"

Kurata was disappointed in Kawai; he suspected the youth had mistaken the attitude Kurata had shown in the hotel lobby as enthusiasm for magic.

Kurata maintained an ill-humored silence. Kawai was flustered now.

"It's a month and a half away, but the tickets are already gone. I have connections, however, so I can still get them."

"Really? But I'm not that interested in it."

"But at this performance he's going to do a new trick. Ikuta Tenkon will attempt the water tank illusion."

Kurata did not respond.

"He enters a tank filled with water, has the top sealed tightly, then escapes from it. An American magician failed when he tried it and died. Which is to say, it's a death-defying trick."

Kurata felt a stir of interest, but his tone of voice was unchanged. It rankled him to think that Kawai might see him as a dyed-in-the-wool fan of magic.

"Let's forget about it."

"I see," Kawai said, dejection in his voice. He hung up.

The next day a special delivery letter arrived from Kawai.

> It pains me to think that I was a little too forward in inviting you to the performance. Just about the only subject that you, *Sensei*—it is only right I call you that—and I can talk about on equal footing is magic. It would appear that I went too far in my excitement at discovering such a topic of conversation.
>
> I am terrible at expressing my feelings. I sometimes think it is perhaps due to the fact that I am a virgin. I think about going somewhere to dispose of this burden, but I am in love with Eiko—the girl at the bar that time—so I have the feeling that would be a kind of sacrilege. Perhaps I am saying too much once again. I frequently feel I don't know what to do with myself. I am nineteen.

KURATA FINALLY WRAPPED UP his work several days later. Relaxed after having made preparations for leaving the hotel, he began perusing the advertising in the newspaper. He saw an ad for a movie he had missed. It was showing at a theater in the flatlands, the same part of town as the bar where he had met Kawai. Young Kawai and the girl Eiko came to mind at the same moment, so he decided he would see the movie, then drop in at the bar. Having just finished his work, a relaxed expansiveness now permitted him to put some time to frivolous use.

He walked through the entertainment district looking for the movie house. It was early evening and getting dark. As he strolled along, lights starting to come on in the rows of stores on either side of the street, he was witness to something entirely unexpected. A man, fiftyish, was walking toward Kurata, his gross belly thrust out before him. Conspicuous were the ruddy face with its rolls of flesh and the bald head. He was apparently a man of wealth, his stride leisurely and self-confident, yet there was something coarse about him.

But the man would not have attracted Kurata's attention had he been by himself. A young woman was following immediately after the man, carrying a fedora chest-high. The sight of this couple struck Kurata as somehow off-kilter.

Both hands carefully on the brim of the fedora, the girl held the hat aloft like some sort of treasure. The hat was brim down, so the peaks created by the crease at the top of the hat came to her chin. The girl's mouth was firmly closed and she walked along, her expression absurdly grave.

Kurata was stunned when he looked at her face.

It was the girl Eiko.

They passed each other, but Eiko, her eyes intent and looking straight ahead, did not notice him. He stopped and looked back.

Kurata had no idea why the man remained hatless and had the girl follow holding his hat. Nonetheless, judging from their posture, one could see the vague outline of their relationship. They were not, of course, father and daughter. It was clear that the couple had a physical relationship and that it was based on money. You could say that what Kurata saw was a paradigm that a master and his young mistress would create.

Kurata imagined the scene a little earlier. "My head's steaming. Here, hold onto this," the man would have said, taking off his hat as he stood in the street and handed it to the girl. He would have taken out a handkerchief from his pocket and wiped his bald head, unconcerned that people might be watching, then resumed his bold stride. The girl would have followed on his heel holding the hat.

He had seen the movie and was now a bit hesitant, but it was that very hesitancy that strengthened Kurata's determination to head for the bar.

The girl stood behind the bar, her face fair and immaculate. He spoke to that face.

"Eiko, I don't suppose Kawai will come tonight, will he."

"He was here just yesterday, so I don't think he'll come to-night. But I'm surprised you remembered my name."

"I know it. And other things as well."

The image of the girl walking along with the hat at chest level came to Kurata. He then imagined Kawai and the girl together. He saw her standing next to Kawai. She was holding his silk hat at her breast, upside down.

Kawai, in tails, sticks his hand into the hat and draws out a white rabbit. He draws out a dove, a goldfish bowl filled with water, a red parasol. He withdraws a bouquet of roses and, on bended knee, gives it to the girl. Reaching further into his hat, his hand pulls out the bald-headed man with the ruddy face. The man fixes a disdainful eye on Kawai, who stands there with a bemused expression on his face. Then the man thrusts his jaw toward Kawai and signals to the girl, walking away without a word. The girl throws down the silk hat she's been holding with two hands as though she's grabbed a hot pan with her bare hands. She follows the man, walking off with a most serious look on her face.

This was the scene that flashed instantaneously through Kurata's brain. The girl stared wordlessly at Kurata. It struck him as curious that the silence was not awkward.

"Kawai says he's nineteen."

"Yes."

"How old are you?"

"Eighteen."

"Aha, a boy and a girl."

"Well, Kawai is certainly a boy."

"You're right. Calling Kawai a boy is, of course, closer to the mark, isn't it. There's something lovable about him."

"But he's too lovable."

"It's a problem for a kid to be too lovable, is it?"

"It is. A boy's got to be almost hateful. Somebody you can't rely on."

"For a girl, however, it's naturally best to be lovable, almost. Right?"

She gave Kurata a quick, questioning look.

KURATA THOUGHT ABOUT KAWAI from time to time. And he also thought, with a certain measure of anxiety, about whether Kawai would become aware of the girl's secret, and if he did, when it would happen.

Kawai phoned a month later.

"*Sensei*, it's me, Kawai."

Kawai's voice sounded different from the voice Kurata remembered.

"Kawai? You mean the one who was so good at magic?"

"Yes."

"Your voice doesn't sound the same."

"Is that so? But it is indeed me."

His tone was serious. There was a slight pause, then he continued.

"*Sensei*, can I get you to come to my lodgings this coming Sunday afternoon?"

Irritated, Kurata fell silent at what he considered the youth's obtrusiveness. Perhaps picking up on this, Kawai hurried on.

"This is a brazen-faced request, but I should very much like it if you would come. I'll no longer make such requests of you. This is my last one."

"I go to your lodgings and then what happens?"

"I'd like you to see a trick I've devised. I've perfected the old water tank trick. I should like someone of standing to verify that I will be doing it half a month before Ikuta Tenkon's performance."

"Aha, the water tank trick, is it? And my role will be just to verify?"

"No, it won't be only that," he said, pausing. "I'm having only you and Eiko watch."

His voice lacked animation; to the contrary, it struck Kurata as depressed. But he decided there are also instances when your excitement is at a high level and so, paradoxically, you feel a coolness that curiously suppresses excitement.

"Well, all right," Kurata responded, "I'll be there."

That Sunday Kurata instinctively halted at the entrance to Kawai's room as he was about to go in. Inside a large, square wooden box sat on the tatami, and for an instant it seemed to him to fill the entirety of the small four-and-a-half mat room. When he had gotten over his surprise he could see the box was not that big. It was about the size of a square one-man *furo* tub. He saw Eiko in the space left, the only space the box did not occupy.

"We're the only observers?" he asked Kawai.

"Two are enough. Two observers, both of whom were dragged here against their will."

"Even so, you've made yourself a huge contraption, haven't you."

"I borrowed leftover lumber from work and made it myself."

"But what will happen to Ikuta Tenkon if you succeed with this water tank stunt? It's a good two weeks before his performance, isn't it?"

"Actually this feat is not the sort that can be performed on the stage. It is enough for me to have you two see it."

The girl, not saying a word, listened as Kurata and Kawai talked, an ambiguous smile on her lips. She could well have been seeing Kawai's behavior as childish or perhaps felt it a nuisance.

Kawai removed the cover from the box. Water filled it to the brim.

"Please look inside. You'll find neither tricks nor gimmicks."

The bottom of the box was visible through the water. In the subdued light of the room you could only vaguely estimate the distance between the bottom of the box and the surface of the water. Kurata guessed there was enough room for a double bottom.

"I am going into the box and close the lid over me. If I were to do it right now, water would overflow onto the tatami, so I will now ladle out that portion of water."

Kawai lowered a small bucket into the water and dumped the water he scooped out into the garden; he repeated this several times.

"As you might expect, it would not do to have you watch too close to the box, so please get back, as close as possible to the wall."

The girl and Kurata stood with their backs against the wall. Kawai took the wooden cover and showed them how it was to be set over the box.

"Normally I would have an assistant put on the cover when I got inside and fasten the latches on the outside. The latches are attached here."

He showed how to lower the metal clasps attached to the edge of the cover and insert them into the fittings at the side of the box. The fittings, one each, were mounted below the four on the cover.

"Ei-*chan*, I'd like you to take the place of the assistant and perform that function, doing it like this," he said, not taking his eyes off the girl.

She nodded, saying nothing.

"I shall now begin."

Kawai had not taken off his clothes. For an instant his eyes seemed to burn with a fierce intensity; the color drained from his face, leaving it deathly pale.

"Ei-*chan*, I want you yourself to securely fasten the latches. In five minutes you'll see me standing by the tree in the garden."

Kurata looked in the direction the youth was pointing and saw a tall, spindly tree in a corner of the small garden. The sun was just then at the very top of the tree; behind a thin haze of cloud it had lost its brightness and was an orange disk.

Kawai stepped over the edge of the box and slowly lowered himself into the water. There was the ponderous slosh and swash of the water as it rose in the box, stopping just short of the brim. The girl placed the cover on the box and fastened the latches at the four corners. The movement of her hands was methodical.

Kurata looked at the clock. Two minutes had passed. He decided that it must be set up so that Kawai could pass through the water and escape between the bottom and a side. He squatted down and peered at the bottom of the box. It was then that he realized there were short wooden legs at each of the four corners and that he was looking into the space between the bottom of the box and the tatami.

If Kawai's able to escape from this box, Kurata thought, *he's a genius, superior even to Ikuta Tenkon*. But in the next instant it suddenly struck him.

That's impossible.

His hands swiftly went to the latches.

"Kawai realized what you were doing, eh?"

"What?"

"The guy you're with. The older, bald one with the money."

Her face, eyes wide, was right in front of his. Even as he spoke his hands continued to quickly unfasten the latches. And he recalled the motion of her hands when she tightly secured, completely without emotion, these same latches.

Kurata pulled the semi-conscious Kawai from the box. Rivulets of water ran off his body and pattered onto the tatami. Kurata gave Kawai's cheek, plastered with wet hair, several rapid slaps. The youth's eyes half opened, then quickly closed. A sheepish expression spread across his face and disappeared.

"Kawai," the girl snapped, "you're such a fool."

She immediately regained her composure: "You're truly a fool."

Her voice was so cold Kurata could not stop himself from staring at her.

A month later Kurata received a letter from Kawai.

> In the end, I did not feel like going to see Ikuta Tenkon's performance. Since then I have been knocking about the backstreets of Shinjuku and Asakusa almost every night. I can now draw from memory a map of the Hanazono-chō quarter.[2] One night, after walking around until very late, I stayed at a flophouse near the south side of the station and the next day resumed my wandering. On a street corner a middle-aged woman laughed at me and told me to drop in at her place, that I had a cute face. I laughed right back at her, but in fact in my heart of hearts I was terrified. I had boasted to my workmates that I would most certainly lose my virginity by the time I was twenty, but when the opportunity presented itself, I was terrified. I am like an ox that cannot eat because it is tethered, though his feed is right in front of him. No, in my case it is certainly not a rope. Around me everyone is doing fine; only I am irritated, irritated at being left behind. To make matters worse, a man and woman live in the room next to mine. Late at night I hear voices making strange sounds; it almost drives me over the edge. They make me want to barge into their place and knock them down. A man at my company three years older than me hinted that sex is 'really something special.' It is as though I am caught in a crossfire.

> *Sensei* is a very busy person and I have for you only tiresome stories to tell, so I believe I am nothing but an annoyance for you. I shall not see you again until the day I can talk with you on an equal footing, having received an education of some sort and accumulated a good deal of experience. I truly apologize for the other day. It embarrasses me.

When Kurata had finished reading the letter he slowly returned it to the envelope.

"There are indeed times like this," he muttered to himself.

---

2 An area east of Shinjuku station; the name was officially dropped in 1973.

Hydrangeas

紫陽花

Translated by Lawrence Rogers

THE GROUND IN THE heart of the city is either completely paved over or buried under buildings of steel and concrete, making it something of a problem to actually see the naked earth.

When he was a child—that was a good thirty years ago—there was a lot of earth to be seen. His home, a wood-frame house, had stood on an open triangle of ground well over three hundred meters square. Two things commonplace then and only rarely encountered now are earth and horses. If you stood at the front gate and watched the street, it wasn't long before a horse pulling a wagon or one bearing a soldier would happen along. To see a horse nowadays you have to go to the zoo, the circus or a racetrack. All sorts of trees and shrubs grew on the part of the land the house was not built on, which is to say, in the garden. Crape myrtle blossomed pink by a gigantic, aged plum tree and in a corner flower bed in the garden weeds flourished in the stead of flowers.

"The hydrangeas have big flowers, don't they," he observed.

The old woman sat up in the futon spread out in the middle of the dimly-lit room.

"Hydrangeas are not the sort of things you want in your garden."

"Why not, Grandma?"

The old woman, who had lost the use of her legs, had been confined to her bed for many years. The cause of her affliction remained a mystery despite countless examinations.

"Because they're supposed to be bad luck."

"How would they be bad luck, I wonder?"

"How, my dear? It means something unlucky will happen."

"Then should we pull them up?"

"Makes no sense at this point. They were here when we moved in, you know."

"You didn't pull them up when you moved in because you didn't know they're bad luck?"

"It's not that I didn't know. I just don't believe that sort of thing."

The boy was silent.

"Misfortune—it's everywhere and happens all the time."

The boy said nothing for a few moments.

"But why are they bad luck?"

"Why, indeed. Say, you know what the big tree by the hydrangeas is?"

"Someone said it's a boxwood tree."

"Do you know what kind of wood boxwood is?"

"What do you mean 'what kind'?"

"It's used to make women's combs. It's really something for a boxwood tree to get that big."

THE WAR BEGAN AT last and soon turned into a grand-scale affair. Just before American planes began flying through the city skies, his grandmother fell ill and died.

His home burned to the ground soon after, victim of an incendiary bomb from an American plane, but his was not the only house destroyed. As he stood in the ruins of his home, there lay before him a houseless expanse of black ground as far as the eye could see.

The war ended and several years passed. He was not able, however, to return to where he had once lived. One needed a good deal of money to build even a small house.

He and his mother were renting a room. His father had died ten years before.

Waist-high weeds flourished over the whole of the triangular lot. The boxwood tree his grandmother had been so proud of was now a charred stump buried in the weeds. Two or three sunflowers, taller than a man, were in bloom, their rich yellow flower-heads facing skyward. He didn't think there had been sunflowers in the garden before. He had no idea where the seeds might have come from.

The coloring of the sunflowers struck him as gross. The yellow of the petals seemed too rich and the burnt umber seeds were much too overdeveloped. The overall effect of the plants was of damp powder, and it clung to his soul.

He had never felt that way about sunflowers until then. Perhaps he was affronted by these flowers standing with their heads held high on land that he wanted to return to but couldn't.

"Insufferable damned flowers!" he muttered to himself as he started walking. He stood on the sidewalk and looked back, the street now between him and the lot.

"It's an unlucky flower," he muttered once again, sensing something from the past about to surface. Then he remembered what his grandmother had said as she looked at the hydrangeas.

Hydrangeas are not the sort of things you want in your garden.

Yet why were they considered to be bad luck? Grown up now, he turned it over in his mind. Maybe it's because they're grown in cemeteries a lot, he thought as he directed his gaze at the sunflowers.

It's as though they're growing right on top of a corpse.

It wasn't just their color that made him think that about the sunflowers, but also, he suspected, because they had sprung up from seeds from who knows where in ground laid waste by incendiary bombs.

"A corpse lies buried beneath the sunflower stalks."

He had heard that phrase somewhere before. It was much like the opening of a short story by Kajii Motojirō: "A corpse lies buried beneath the cherry tree."[1] When you examine the blossoms individually you can see that the petals are small and faintly tinted. And when many of these trees are in full bloom together, obscuring an entire hill, you're overcome by the eeriness of the scene: it's like having a chloroformed handkerchief waved under your nose. As Kajii put it, it's a kind of mysterious ambiance, "like a well-spun top in a perfectly stationary spin."

It was precisely for that reason that he sensed a putrefying corpse beneath the tree. A putrefying corpse swarming with maggots, out of which, however, "dripped a crystal-clear fluid."

The sunflower suggested a corpse more directly. A putrid, worm-covered corpse in the process of congealing into a turbid, pasty fluid.

Then what would a corpse buried under the leaves of the hydrangeas be like?

The hydrangea flower forms a corolla of a mass of small, single-leaf petals. Its bright purple color does not stain the plucking fingers. And some are a whitish, faded purple. They suggest dried sweets and dried fruit.

This would seem to be neither a putrefying corpse nor a corpse oozing pellucid fluid. Could the ground beneath the hydrangea hold a mummy in a casket, or perhaps a bleached skeleton which long ago lost any trace of flesh?

---

1 This quotation and the two that follow it are from the literary vignette "Beneath the Cherry Tree" (Sakura no ki no shita ni wa) by the miniaturist Kajii Motojirō (1901–1932), published in 1928. Accessible at http://www.aozora.gr.jp/cards/000074/files/427_19793.html

IT DID NOT LOOK as though they would be able to return to the triangle of land. Simply making ends meet took all of their energy. He was in college, but he found all sorts of jobs and rarely went to classes.

He was unhappy with this state of affairs and went one day to sell the land to a broker. He stood in the office doorway and chatted with a shrewd-looking middle-aged woman. The figure she gave him for the land was not even a third of what he had anticipated. If that were all he could get, he would simply be throwing his money away on the installment plan for day-to-day living expenses. He decided not to sell it and left.

A man had recently proposed marriage to his mother. The man, who was her age, had also lost his spouse to illness several years earlier. His mother rejected the proposal.

"It'd be too much of a bother now," she said. She had lived the decade of her thirties as a widow.

"Don't say that," he told her. "Why don't you think about it?"

Her resolve, however, was firm, unexpectedly so.

"Besides," she would say, "I'm no longer a woman." She had had surgery for a uterine tumor the year before, and they had removed her ovaries as well.

"Don't talk like that."

His mother had something else to discuss with him.

"Mr. Abe is asking us to let him have 40 per cent of the property." Abe was the gentleman proposing marriage to his mother.

"What will he do with the land if he buys it?"

"It would appear he wants to build a house to live in."

"Surely he already has his own house, doesn't he?"

"I think he wants to dispose of it and live on the land he buys from us."

"Then, Mother," he counseled, with no sarcasm intended, "you could simply move right into his place."

"No, I don't want to. It'd be too much of a bother."

"Well then, what's to be done?"

"It seems that he's already sold the house he's living in."

"Which is to say," he said with a nod, "if you don't let him have the land, Mr. Abe will be left hanging."

He told her he would at least meet with Mr. Abe. He was more than inclined to take on the role of go-between for his mother and the man.

Mr. Abe was a courteous, middle-aged gentleman. He was a tall, good-looking man, but he either was unaware of his good looks or was hobbled by a failure of will that left him innocent of their use. Any link between Mr. Abe and the assertiveness he would have needed to dispose of the house he was living in eluded him, but the man did seem to be a suitable person for his mother should she re-marry.

He settled on a price with Mr. Abe and let him have part of the land.

He would not have had enough money to build his little forty-square-meter home with the sum Mr. Abe paid him had he not borrowed a roughly equivalent amount elsewhere.

The Abe home was built first, then half a year later his house was built next to it.

The weeds on the triangular lot were cut, exposing the dark earth. He planted several trees. A slender pear tree bore tiny fruit.

Gardenias, the broad-leaf aralia, and five hydrangeas. It was autumn, so he saw no blossoms on them. All of these had been transplanted from Mr. Abe's garden.

A month later he discovered something unexpected in a corner of the garden. Dozens of slender trunks protruded from the ground around the boxwood tree, now burned away to a black stump. Small tongue-shaped leaves clearly showed that the trunks, so slender they ought better be called stems, were boxwood. The branches of the boxwood had come alive again, and its shoots were pressing their faces up through the earth.

He was astounded at the tenacity of its roots. That it had needed three years to regain enough strength to push its slender trunks above ground made him all the more aware of this tenacity.

Returning to the house, he had some advice for his mother.

"How about moving next door now?"

She was wavering, and he had more to say to her.

"I'll fill in the rest of the family for you. I'll explain the situation simply."

He had not the slightest feeling he was losing his mother. He believed she would, in the end, be happier this way and he, for his part, would not have to worry about her. Still, having displayed such solicitude, he found himself feeling old beyond his years. He had just dropped out of college and started work in a job he had found for himself.

His mother moved next door, and he installed Makiko, a young woman he had been on familiar terms with for some time, in his house. This was nothing remotely resembling the gaudy spectacle of marriage. There was no marriage ceremony nor did he have her name added to the official family register.

Some months later he discovered Makiko had taken it upon herself to go down to the ward office and put her name on the family register.

Well, that's all right too, he told himself.

He didn't call Makiko by her name. That did not mean, of course, she had a pet name that he used. He signaled his intention to have her do something by uttering a quick, growl-like sound.

His friends called to their girlfriends, lovers and fiancées in all sorts of ways.

"Yōko!"

"Yes, dear."

"O-sei!"

"What is it?"

"Bambi!"

"Yeah?"

Hearing these exchanges, he was assailed by embarrassment and, simultaneously, something akin to sorrow. He put it down to youth that embarrassment should vanish when this sort of summons rose in his friends' throats. For his part, however, he was absolutely incapable of calling Makiko by her name.

The seasons changed. It was now early summer, and the hydrangeas in the garden blossomed into their corolla blooms. They were a vivid purple. He turned his gaze on them only for an instant and did not let it linger there.

TEN YEARS PASSED. HE was still living in the same small house with Makiko. Friends had predicted they would not last a year together.

Once a relationship had lasted that long there was something in him that made an effort to continue on with it, that carefully tried to maintain an equilibrium and keep things together somehow, no matter how predisposed to self-destruction the alliance. This something might have been bound up with loyalty or with a streak of rusticity in his make-up.

After ten years he was now able, he thought, to have Makiko's existence assume the commonality of the air he breathed. Success, he concluded.

He did not realize it is mere illusion to think one can transform another human being with her own independent individuality into an air-like entity.

Makiko, however, was so inured to her airy role she sustained the illusion. Food that he fancied eating was arrayed on his table as if by magic. He could even invite friends over and set off openly for a night of drinking and wenching.

"You've really got her trained."

That's what his friends said, and only half in jest. It was his intention to live an easeful life. Sometimes, however, he would be plunged abruptly into intense discontent.

He would be walking along the street. He would catch sight of a woman and be attracted to her. There would be a man at her side. He would detect the flush of pride in the man's face—see it glowing there—and he would be filled with envy and jealousy. He would decide the woman was more suited to him, that he would never experience that glow as long as he lived.

It was at just such a time that he met Chieko.

She began phoning him frequently. She had no real reason for calling him. They did not know each other that well, so they soon found it difficult to make idle chatter. The silences on the line were awkward, and he would toss off the first thing that came to mind.

"Come on over sometime."

"But I have to have a reason of some sort."

"You don't need any reason."

"I know! You get sick. Then I'll pay you a sick call."

It was Chieko, by and large, who telephoned.

"I passed your house yesterday in my car."

"I'm surprised you knew where it was."

"I knew. You told me where you were the last time I talked to you. There were lots of hydrangeas blooming in the garden."

"Then it was probably my house."

"The purple was so pretty. They seem so big compared with regular hydrangeas."

"I rather doubt it. They're just ordinary hydrangeas."

"Listen, would you give me one of them?"

He didn't answer.

"You have a lot, don't you?"

"I don't have that many. Of course, I have no objection at all to giving you some."

Quite suddenly he was uttering his long-gone grandmother's words.

"But they say you'll have bad luck if you plant hydrangeas in your garden."

Chieko said nothing for a few moments. His statement must have seemed abrupt.

"Then why are they in your garden?"

"That sort of thing doesn't bother me."

"It doesn't bother me either," Chieko said in a burst of laughter.

He suspected she didn't particularly want the hydrangea. It had just come up in the course of the conversation.

He still had the five hydrangea plants in the garden. The flowers' season was at last past and the plants were now just green leaves. Saw-tooth notches edged the leaves.

"COME ON, GIVE ME a hydrangea."

Chieko was calling again.

"You really want one?"

"I really do. That's why I've been asking you for one."

"But they say you shouldn't plant hydrangeas in your garden."

He wondered why he was telling her that again and was momentarily silent.

"I don't care about that."

"Then I'll bring it over in a day or two."

"You will? You've never been to my place, have you. Bring it over and stay a while."

He hung up.

"Chieko says she wants a hydrangea plant," he told Makiko.

"Let her have one."

"I'll take it over within the next few days."

"Then I'll get one ready so you can take it over whenever you want."

"The small plant by the front door is nice and compact. It had big flowers, as I recall, so that'll be the one."

One night several days later he hailed a cab on the street in front of the house. Makiko kept him waiting for some time, the taxi door wide open. She appeared from behind the house with a hydrangea, struggling with the obviously heavy plant. She had wrapped its roots in newspaper and bound its spreading branches with cord. The plant was as tall as she was.

"That's awfully big, don't you think?"

"They're all about this size."

He shifted his gaze next to the front door. The hydrangea plant was still standing there.

"Why didn't you take that plant?"

"It would be obvious if I dug that one up, like a missing front tooth. I took one from the back. Hydrangeas are all the same. You'd better get it to her right away."

Makiko's eyes seemed to be laughing, and he sensed a curious elation in her. He did not have time, however, to dwell on the nature of this elation. He quickly carried the plant into the cab.

The hydrangea was terribly unwieldy and took up most of the back seat. Its branches were badly bent, the tips pressed up against the inside of the window. He found himself pushed into a corner of the seat. The driver spoke to him a little while after they started off.

"That's a big plant, sir. What kind is it?"

"It's a hydrangea. Somebody asked me for one."

"A hydrangea. Imagine that."

"You don't sound very enthusiastic. I suppose you think it's bad luck, eh?"

"Bad luck? No, I don't know anything about it being bad luck. I just thought it's not the sort of plant you would ask someone for."

"Uh-huh, well, you're right there."

"No offense meant, of course."

"No problem."

"But you should have lopped off those branches, I think. It would have been less trouble if you'd cut it down to the root."

"You're right about that."

The cabby liked to talk and went from one topic to another.

"Taxi drivers work one day and get the next off, don't they?" he finally broke in. "It's a surprisingly good set up, I'd say."

"It's not that good. You're too tired to do a darned thing. On top of which, I'm newly married. I just got married!"

"Then on your day off you can spend all day in bed."

"I do that and there's no way I can work the next day. But I admit, sir, being newly married isn't half bad."

"Isn't it?"

That had caught him off guard.

"Not bad at all. On my day off yesterday we did *origami* all day."

"Paper-folding?"

"You know the sailboat one, do you? 'All right now, close your eyes and take hold of the tip of the sail. All right now, open your eyes.' When you open your eyes, you see that you're holding the stern, not the tip like you thought. It really fascinates me, no matter how many times I do it."

"You don't say."

"'All right now, take hold of the tip of the sail!'"

There was a small cluster of shops across from the suburban train station. Chieko, in a red sweater, was standing in front of a fruit store on the corner.

He had the driver stop in front of her. The brightly lit interior of the fruit store behind Chieko dazzled his eyes. The skin of the green apples and of the yellow tangerines shone sleekly under the bright lights of the store.

He rolled down the window and called out to her, his head sticking out from between the leaves of the hydrangea.

"There's no room for you in the back seat."

"Oh dear, it's all leaves."

Chieko looked at him, her eyes dark and intense.

The tip of a slender branch that was bent against the window suddenly whipped out through the opening, forcing its leaves to brush, chin-first, over his face.

"I'll ride next to the driver."

She then proceeded to tell the driver the way to her house.

FIVE YEARS PASSED.

He and Makiko and Chieko had grown weary of the triangular relationship that bound them together.

"And the hydrangea . . .," Chieko began one night, as though she had suddenly remembered the plant.

"The hydrangea? Oh, the hydrangea plant."

There had been precious little time to think about the hydrangeas those five years.

"Was there, by any chance, a hydrangea in your garden that had never bloomed?"

"Why?"

"That hydrangea, you said that Makiko had dug it up. I can't help thinking she picked one that wouldn't bloom."

"It hasn't bloomed?"

"Not once."

"Maybe it's because it was transplanted into new soil."

The hugeness of the hydrangea Makiko had carried to the taxi, its door wide open. And her curious elation. The laughter in her eyes. These recollections oppressed him with their eeriness. He wanted to push them out of his mind, and thus he had mentioned the soil. Actually, he was in complete, albeit silent, agreement with what Chieko was saying.

"It's been five years now," she said.

"Five years!"

"Makiko would do something like that, wouldn't she."

"But," he said, "it's just as well the hydrangea doesn't bloom."

"You mean because it's bad luck? If it doesn't bloom we'll have no bad luck?"

"I'm not worried about bad luck. But there's something unreal about that plant."

Chieko took these statements as a defense of Makiko. Her nostrils flared and her mood took a turn for the worse.

The following year he moved out of his house and began living with Chieko. One morning Chieko, who had been looking out into the garden, suddenly cried out.

"Look! The hydrangea's in bloom!"

A single corolla, bright purple, was visible amongst the green leaves.

"I didn't notice it blooming yesterday," he said. "Looks just as though someone came along with a single flower and put it there for display."

"Do you suppose this year it's finally gotten used to the soil?"

He gazed wordlessly at the hydrangea, its delicate petals massed together into a floral crown.

Is something about to happen? Is something buried in the earth beneath the plant? Does this mean a flattened, shriveled corpse lies buried there?

A breeze blew and bright purple swayed amidst the leaves of green.

I Ran Over a Cat

猫踏んじゃった

Translated by Lawrence Rogers

It was a Sunday afternoon in midsummer, but the heat of day was uncommonly dry. A broad street sloped down the hill in front of Mikami Sōichi's house, its surface reflecting the rays of the sun and shimmering white before him.

A gravel-covered yard fronted the entrance to the house. When he opened the door of his car, parked in the yard, he was struck full in the face by an outflow of searing air. The car, having absorbed an ample measure of the sun's rays, was as hot as a baker's oven. He got into the driver's seat, put the vehicle into gear, and began to ease it backward out through the wooden gateway.

There was a sidewalk between the street and the gate, so he moved the car along at a crawl, head turned around and alert for pedestrians.

He expected to see neither people nor cars. The white sloping street shimmered in the sun. The rear wheels left the edge of the sidewalk for the roadway, a drop of several inches he wouldn't have felt if he hadn't been waiting for it.

He was used to this, but this time he sensed something vaguely different in the car's movement. In that instant the figure of a man suddenly appeared in the rear window, wobbled erratically, and just as quickly disappeared from view. He jerked the hand brake back as far as it would go and jumped out of the car.

A bicycle with a large, squarish box on its rack lay toppled in the road, and next to it on the ground was a young man. His face, dark-complexioned, suggested he might be the combative sort.

Mikami ran over to the man and, arm around his shoulder, raised him to a sitting position and awaited the torrent of abuse that was sure to come.

At the same time, a part of him said, *No, it won't happen.* The thought occurred to him that his car had not knocked over the bicycle and its rider.

"Are you all right?"

As he asked the question he could feel the strength drain from the man's body, which sagged heavily against his encircling arm. This was only for an instant, however; the man immediately regained his strength. Mikami noticed the beads of sweat that covered his forehead. He could not account for them, but he sensed something even stranger at the edge of his field of vision as he peered into the other man's face.

He shifted his gaze to the sloping roadway.

Something wet and clammy, with mucous-like ridges and furrows, covered the ground right next to where the man had fallen. For the briefest moment he had no idea what it was. Its color was dark, somber and wet, not the sort of color one encounters in everyday life. What was normally hidden from view deep within the mammalian body lay out on the pavement, as though it had been dumped into the street or casually set down there.

A cat's innards, together with its bloody serosity, were spread wide over the dry surface of the road. He knew it was a cat because a cat's head lay at the side of the expanse of wetness. Its face, tiny compared to the area taken up by its internal organs on the street, lay off all by itself.

"What the hell happened?"

His gaze alternated between the man's forehead and the large wet splotch on the road.

"Are you okay?" Mikami asked again as the man regarded him wordlessly. He was not really focussing on Mikami. The man nodded slowly, however, and picked up his bicycle.

No words of reproach issued from the man's mouth. He cast a furtive glance at the roadway, then began walking, pushing the bicycle at his side. He walked up the hill. His figure gradually grew more distant.

Only a very short time had elapsed since he had helped the man sit up, yet it seemed to him each movement was an image projected in slow motion.

As the man began to recede into the distance, Mikami was at last able to digest what had happened. The cat had been in the road when the wheels dropped down off the sidewalk. There's a Japanese jelly candy that comes wrapped in a balloon-like wrapper. When you squeeze the rubber-encased ball of candy, the contents explode into the palm. The cat's innards, put under sudden and extreme pressure and having no relief from that pressure, had burst *en masse* from the abdomen.

Had the man seen this happen?

As Mikami had suspected, it was not his car that had bowled over the man on the bicycle. It was the sight that suddenly presented itself to him as he was coming up the hill, leaning forward over his handlebars and pedaling laboriously, that had done it.

Mikami recalled the expression on the man's face, an expression of bewilderment that denied the abrupt spectacle was to be credited.

And yet why did the agile little creature not move out of the way of the wheel of the slowly approaching car? He looked down at the ground once more. The wet, sticky, reeking ground seemed almost alive. Mikami was bewildered. He felt that an absurd situation had been suddenly thrust upon him. Mikami recalled what a poet had said about cats—they don't come when you call them, yet come when you don't—and he felt his attitude shamelessly harden. He had no intention of disposing of the corpse, in any case. First of all, it wasn't a corpse. It was a strange thing quite apart from that. But he didn't know what it might be.

I'd better get out of here.

He stole a quick look around him. He sensed that several pairs of eyes were fixed on him. He wanted to walk over to where the eyes were and ask them what they had seen.

Instead he concluded once again that he should make himself scarce. He returned to his car and sped away, going up the hill. He returned home several hours later, back to the scene of the crime. The sloping street was bright and dry in the sun, but now there was a dark patch on the surface of the shimmering street. The area was certainly dry, but shrouded in black. The cat was tiny bits of flattened flesh sticking to the pavement.

No one disposed of the animal. The tires of the many cars that ran up the hill effected the clean-up. All that remained of the viscera that had covered the street was a faint stain.

SEVERAL YEARS WENT BY. From time to time the memory of the sloping street that midsummer day would present itself to Mikami Sōichi.

The unpleasant part of that recollection seemed, without his knowing it, to be abandoned, left behind, and the scope of memory gradually narrowed.

The sloping street shimmering white in the midsummer sun. The cat's innards on the hard, dry pavement, as though someone had suddenly set them down there. The harsh sun shining on the still quick intestines, just torn from the abdominal cavity. The guts exposed that very instant, too new even for the flies to have lighted on.

He would be suddenly seized by the need to jump up and run off somewhere. He would wonder if the instant he started running he would feel something swelling inside himself. He had the premonition that this swelling, this thing that resembled the radiance of life, or rather, this unpleasant part that should have disappeared as soon as he began running, was about to wrap itself around him. If this happened he would no doubt have to keep running for a while, screaming a meaningless scream.

The part you don't call comes to you.

He would eagerly adopt the posture of flight.

In fact, however, just as these recollections rose to his consciousness without the slightest warning, they likewise, even after surfacing, brought no change in his day-to-day existence. Each day came and went like the one before it. The recollections were perilous, but a part of him longed for the peril.

One night Mikami Sōichi was walking through the evening streets with a friend.

"What'll we do?"

"How 'bout a drink?"

"You wanna go to a bar?"

"Bars are a drag."

"So where you wanna go?"

"What the hell. Let's go to a bar."

"I've got it!" said his friend, volunteering the name of a watering hole with a hint of malice in his face, "Let's go to The Robin." He knew about Mikami and Misako. It wasn't that Mikami and Misako had a special relationship. Mikami was infatuated with the woman, but she had sharply rejected all his advances.

Mikami forced a smile: "The Robin?"

"You're not in love with her or anything, are you?"

"No, it's just that . . ."

"Then what difference does it make? It's no big deal. You're expecting too much if you're not in love with her and yet want it to be a big deal anyway."

"Right you are."

Mikami gave easy concurrence, so his friend took another tack. It's a bore to have someone docilely agree with you when you're trying to needle him.

"And yet, what do you suppose it's like to be in love?"

"What, indeed."

"Maybe you feel as though your guts are jumping right up into your throat."

"That might sum it up."

"I'll bet that's just how you feel if you've led a sexless life for a long time, then find yourself face to face with a woman."

"Really? I suppose so."

"You're pretty noncommittal. Will your guts rise up when you see Misako?"

Mikami didn't respond.

"But I hear Misako's not the sort of woman who won't let you have your way with her unless she loves you. A guy who said he went to her apartment told me her place was a strew-mess."

"A 'strew-mess'?'"

"He said it didn't do it justice to just say her place was a mess. The whole place was like a big trash can, and she was lolling right in the middle of it. She's fastidious about her person at work, so when I heard that I was perversely attracted to her."

"And the guy who went to her apartment, he wasn't you?"

"Uh-oh! Are you in love with her?"

"Love or not, I can still get jealous. It is, to put it simply, a question of pride."

"Anyway," his friend responded, "let's go to The Robin."

At the bar he found Misako was, uncharacteristically, well into her cups. Her eyes shone darkly. Her dusky skin was deeply flushed, and this excited Mikami.

"You're drunk," he said to her.

"You think so?"

"Your face is red."

"Yeah, I've got a buzz on. When I get drunk my body gets red all over, tip to toe."

The rawness of the words goaded Mikami. She pushed her body into his back as he sat on the high bar stool, the swell of a breast against his elbow

"It's so hot." She pressed her palms against her cheeks, and eyes upturned, stared at him. The teasing light in her eyes commingled with the feeble light of the club as her lips spread gradually into a smile. It was a provocative smile, so incredibly broad it seemed to crease her face from ear to ear.

She looks like a cat, he thought.

Her breast was against his arm again. It pressed against him, and he could feel it moving, and its firmness.

Women and cats: they come when you haven't called them, and when you do, they ignore you.

The woman sitting on the stool between Mikami and his friend turned to her.

"I want you to hand over the kitten. Don't lie to me, hear?"

Misako did not respond, but wrapped her arms around Mikami's waist as she stood behind him.

"Let's go someplace when the bar closes," she said to him.

"Listen, you're giving me the cat. Understand? Right?" Her tone was brusque, and the look in her eyes sharp, unwavering. She was ordinarily an even-tempered woman, so this transformation seemed a bit strange. Misako, returning her gaze for an instant, nodded wordlessly, then began rocking Mikami back and forth.

"Let's go someplace!"

The woman next to him spoke again.

"You follow me, right? I'm gonna take it off your hands."

Misako abruptly fell silent when she heard her speak and nodded again.

"What's this about a cat?" Mikami asked. He suspected the cat in question was not really a cat. "Your cat had kittens?"

Silence. When it came to cats, Misako had nothing to say. She seemed even unconcerned, disinterested.

"*You* had the kittens?"

"How could I . . . ?" she began, her response sharp and instantaneous. A glint of anger shone in her dark eyes.

"Why are you getting mad?"

"I'm not mad especially, but . . ."

The woman next to Mikami suddenly started to sing loudly, no doubt to ease the tension. Yet why had this topic of conversation engendered such tension?

"I had a cat! I had a cat!" the woman sang, and Misako soon joined in.

I had a cat. I had a cat. I had a cat. They repeated the phrase over and over.

As she sang Misako once again wrapped her arms around Mikami's waist, rocking him more violently this time.

"Let's go someplace!"

"Where?"

"Come to my apartment."

"Your apartment?"

For a short while Mikami said nothing, but when he spoke he changed the subject.

"Actually, the song goes, 'The cat died,' doesn't it?"

"Right you are," the woman next to him said, and changed the lyrics. "The cat died. The cat died."

"Enough, enough!" Mikami said, then: "You're singing it to a Bayer piece, are you?"[1]

"It's simpler than a Bayer piece. It's simpler than do-re-mi-fa-so."

"La-ti-do, go, kitty, go!"

"Goodness, cats are popping up everywhere, aren't they."

"It can be 'the cat died' or 'I ran over a cat,' or 'I stepped on a cat,'" Mikami's friend offered. "It's 'I stepped on a cat' in all the children's comic books."

1 Josef Bayer (1852–1913), a Viennese composer.

I ran over a cat. I stepped on a cat. The cat died. It was then that the memory of the sloping road in midsummer rose to his consciousness. That had not happened in some time. Just what had that little incident meant to him?

His curiosity aroused, he interrogated his friend.

"In comic books? How's the phrase used?"

"When someone is faking it."

"What do you mean 'faking it'?"

"Which is to say . . . how should I put it? Okay, someone says *popoi-poipoi* or the like to fake words he can't remember, doesn't he. That's what I mean."

"'*Popoi-poipoi*'?"

"You accidentally step on a cat. It'll let out a howl, and you have jolly chaos on your hands. In which case it's closer to the mark to say that you've stepped on a cat, rather than that the cat died."

You can step on a cat's pliant body, Mikami thought to himself, but there's no way he'll die; running over him in your car is a different story, however.

"You're gonna stay 'til closing, right?" he heard his friend say. "I'll be heading home a bit before that."

It was finally closing time.

"Hey, everyone!" Misako shouted to the other women, "Come over to my place. Tomorrow's Sunday. Let's have a rip-roaring good time. Mikami's covering the food for us."

It occurred to Mikami that henceforth whenever he recalled that midsummer road, the memory would inevitably be intertwined with tonight's. His recollection was tarnished before he had been able to make any sense of it. The dry road might shimmer white in the sun, but it would no longer hold any meaning for him.

Mikami recalled the receding figure of the man pushing his bicycle, having wordlessly righted it. He wondered if he should also wordlessly make his getaway. And yet, the man's feelings then were doubtless intense, utterly different from Mikami's now.

An hour later Mikami was in Misako's apartment, together with a half dozen of her co-workers. A store of groceries bought at an all-night market stood in piles on the kitchen table.

"I must say I'm surprised to see the apartment is in ship-shape."

"Dear me," one of the women responded, "you'd been to the old apartment, had you?"

"The old one?"

"You didn't know? She just moved in. Even Misako needs time to make a proper mess."

"You just moved in?" Mikami mumbled.

"What of it?" she said defiantly. Her eyes were cheerless.

"Huh? What do you mean?"

He didn't know why her tone was so defiant.

The cat died.

The cat died.

The women's drunken chorus had begun.

Something Unexpected

不意の出来事

Translated by Lawrence Rogers

YUKIKO'S SKIN DID NOT give off its usual scent. She had just taken off her clothes, but her body was odorless. Usually when her body was hard against mine and covered with a fine film of sweat, I could detect a subtle odor. I was sure that a body damp with the sweat of sexual excitement exuded a delicate aroma.

Once before I had wondered about her odor. A strange powderiness had been intermingled with her half-sweet, half-sour scent. To call it a powdery smell doesn't explain much, but when I got a whiff of it, I felt an awkwardness akin to getting your fingertips smeared with the wing powder of those huge orange moths and not knowing what to do with them. Had I been cool and composed, it would have no doubt struck me as a foul odor, but the smell stirred me sexually, in an abrasively perverse way. Which is to say, the smell held a curious fascination for me, yet I sensed that it was something quite apart from the odors that emanate from the human body.

I had thought the smell a mix of body scent and make-up. I detected the same smell on Yukiko's arms, her side and between her breasts.

"You put eau de cologne all over your body, do you?" I had asked her.

"Of course not. I'm not a rich man's daughter like you see in the movies."

Reflexively, I had looked around the room. This was where I lived, a single nine-square-foot room in a wood-frame apartment building. It got the sun from the west; the tatami was parched yellow.

"Why do you ask?"

"I was wondering about the smell of your skin."

"Dear me, my skin smells?" Yukiko had turned her head sideways on the bed and put her nose against the roundness of her shoulder. I could tell from the flaring of her nostrils she was inhaling deeply.

"You're right. I wonder why? It's an unpleasant smell."

"I wouldn't call it unpleasant. It's as though something in you were sweetly rotting."

My gaze had moved to Yukiko's naked belly, to a twenty-one-year-old's youthfully taut expanse of skin.

"Don't say such awful things." She rested her hands on either side of her navel.

"Well I suppose there's no problem," I said, but my tone sought assurance.

"No problem."

I suspect we both saw the same face in our mind's eye, the face of the thirty-year-old gangster who was Yukiko's lover. Of course, I'd never met him, and I fully intended never to avail myself of the pleasure, so the face that presented itself to me remained indistinct. The only thing about him that was sharply defined was the scar on his left cheek that Yukiko had told me about. His face disappeared, to be replaced by a single jagged green line. In my capacity as reporter for a third-rate weekly news magazine, I had once gone to do a story on photo studios where customers take photos of nude models. In this one studio, part of a *yakuza* organization, a naked girl sat with her thighs spread open. She could not have been twenty, the legal age. I could see a green line snaking down her ash-colored nymphae. It was a bright green, and shone as though applied with luminous paint.

"But I wonder what the smell is," Yukiko said, obviously considering the possibilities. Her dark eyes grew even darker as her thoughts turned inward. Her eyes were one of the things that had attracted me to her.

"It doesn't smell like you."

"My skin shouldn't smell like anything."

"Well then . . ."

"Wait a minute! I've smelled that somewhere before." She was on the verge of remembering, but had apparently gone off in the wrong direction. She bit into her shoulder in annoyance.

Suddenly there was more depth to Yukiko's eyes and they flashed.

"I know! It's an odor that gets into my apartment building from time to time. There's a college lab nearby. From my window I can see students in white coats doing something with test tubes. I'll bet that's where the smell's coming from."

"What kind of research do you suppose they're doing?"

"That I wouldn't know."

Yukiko continued, speaking with assurance.

"Odor is made up of tiny grains. Those grains have insinuated themselves into every pore of my body."

Later, feeling especially close to Yukiko, I went one afternoon to see for myself the area around her apartment building. I had once seen her home to the main entrance, but that had been before I knew she had a lover. The apartment house stood atop a bluff, and a college building, steel and concrete, rose far above the bluff from a spot beneath it. Without calling out to Yukiko, I walked around the apartment house, now and again rubbing the siding with my finger. It was a simple wood-frame apartment building much like the one I was living in. Yukiko had told me she wasn't living with anyone, but the man with the scar on his cheek could well have been in her room. My soul trembled with the tension of danger and my fondness for her.

I stood on the lip of the bluff to gaze on the scene before me. At the time I had completely forgotten about the college lab, but I saw through a glass window right in front of me—surprisingly near—a desk on which stood row after row of test tubes and flasks. I could see several young men in white in the middle of the room.

It wasn't a strong smell, but it was just as Yukiko had said. Little by little the tiny grains of odor clung to the lining of my nose, and when they reached their critical mass I could clearly detect the scent that had risen from Yukiko's skin.

When I smelled that odor on Yukiko, I'd been struck by the fact that it was the antithesis of a human smell. Yet when I faced the white concrete wall and breathed in the odor, it seemed curiously human, almost blood-raw. I stared at the inorganic light of the test tube glass as the young men shook the tubes between their fingertips.

"What the devil sort of research are they doing?" I muttered to myself.

Her skin did not give off any smell. There was no sweat on her body.

"What's the matter?"

She answered immediately, as though she'd been waiting for the opportunity.

"I understand now."

"What?"

"He knows about us."

I pulled away from her.

"What!? Did he follow you here?"

"No. The last time when I left you and returned to the apartment he was waiting for me."

"Just because he was waiting doesn't mean that he knows. He had no proof you'd been with me."

"That's it. There was. Even I hadn't noticed it."

Whenever my body was interlocked with Yukiko's, her face was suffused with tenderness, her expression transformed by a

— 102 —

smile, but when the sexual excitement at last reached its peak, she would shut her eyes tightly and a frown would crease her brow. It was the expression of one in seeming pain. A single deep vertical furrow rose in the space between her eyebrows.

Her expression would return to normal afterward, but the trace of the vertical furrow would remain for several hours. One could have taken it as proof, yet there was no furrow between Yukiko's eyebrows this time. And Yukiko did not sweat, nor did an expression akin to pain come to her face.

"There's no proof left on your face now," I offered.

"I'm worried sick about that. He's going to go see you."

"You told him about me?"

"I had no choice."

Yukiko showed me the bottoms of her feet. Circular welts the size of the nail on a little finger covered her soles. Some were old and had turned purple; others were red and swollen, raw, oozing blisters. I could tell they were wounds caused by crushing out lighted cigarettes on her flesh.

Yukiko was working in a cabaret on the outskirts of the city. That's where I met her. When she was working she wore clothes that exposed much of her shoulders and back. Her lover's way of tormenting her, not injuring those parts of her body needed in her work, terrified me. I saw it as cold audacity, not cautious calculation.

"He might come here now," I said, eyeing the door.

Yukiko lay on the futon, immobilized by her nakedness. For an instant I regarded her suspiciously: was this a set-up? But they couldn't expect to get anything from me, with or without threats.

"He won't come here. He thinks I don't know where you live. I told him where your office is."

"And he's going to work me over?"

"He won't hit you. He's not the kind of guy to use force."

"So why does he want to meet me?"

"Money. No other reason."

"But I don't have any."

"So there's nothing to worry about. You can't get blood from a stone."

I heard this both as an attempt to reassure me and as nonchalance. And I also saw Yukiko's eyes appraising my agitation.

"It's a shame you had to put yourself through this for me," I said, stroking a burn on the bottom of her foot that had turned purple.

I felt like a man dropping a weighted line into the water to plumb its depths.

"No problem. I was happy to suffer for your sake. I was thinking about you the whole while."

Her response did not have its intended effect; my doubt grew all the greater.

What there was no doubt about, however, was that Yukiko's man would be coming to see me. I waited for him, staying in the office as much as possible. He didn't show the next day or the next. As I waited, my imagination worked overtime, creating in my head images of this man of hers I'd yet to meet.

Yukiko had said he was not the sort to resort to violence, and that clearly affected my thinking. It was the young toughs who used force indiscriminately. I decided her boyfriend was a thirty-year-old man of cool and calm demeanor and cold eyes. His frame, clad in a black suit, was lean, as solid as steel, yet supple. Every time they embraced, his body would assuredly raise high ridges of ecstasy on her brow.

Yukiko was not able to break with this man. She acted as though she wanted to free herself, but I suspected that, in fact, she was tied tightly to him, that they were aggressively fashioning a private circle for just the two of them. And was I not being used as a catalyst in the relationship between the two to further strengthen their circle, so that no one could get inside it?

The uneasiness of waiting made me miserable. When I returned to my room I extracted a book of nursery rhymes from the piles of books stacked in my closet and opened to a page at random, running my eyes over the lines of type to divert myself. I often fled from the sordid quotidian into this book I just happened to find at a second-hand bookstore.

The phrase "sordid quotidian" refers, of course, to the nature of my work as a reporter for a third-rate weekly magazine. This is not to say I started out in this calling. When I joined the company it was a publisher of decent books. There was an extremely limited market for such books, however, and most were returned to us. The company changed course. By turning out a magazine carrying salacious articles and exposés, its employees were able, though just barely, to make a living wage.

To reject this sort of work was to starve, the thought of which intimidated me. I did not possess the strength needed to throw it over and launch myself into a new career. I accepted my job, and at night fled to a woman's body or to the pages of the nursery rhyme collection.

My eyes moved over the book of rhymes as I gleaned bits here, pieces there.

Laugh!
Laugh!
Laugh while you can!

or

The sky is deep blue,
the air so mild;
faint shadows on the path
and the sun shines in the wild.

or

Pease porridge hot,
pease porridge cold,
pease porridge in a pot nine days old.

My eyes came to rest on the title "Something Unexpected." The poem beneath it went as follows:

The crane,
graceful as a woman,
always took its meals
with a knife and fork.
How refined,
the sight of it!
until one day
it ate the cork.

A tortoise-shell kitten slept
inside a hat
and thought it
a very fine bed,
but, alas,
a near-sighted man,
unawares,
suddenly put it on his head.

My heart mellowed before this drollery. The drollery, however, took on a mocking tone. A contemptuous gleam appeared in the cold eyes that Yukiko's boyfriend fixed on me. Rubbing his forefinger lightly against the tip of his nose, he bore down on me with long strides. . . .

I reconsidered: was this episode really something that had caught me by surprise? A part of me had been uneasy ever since I learned that a *yakuza* had attached himself to Yukiko. I can say that it was not "something unexpected" for me. At the least, I was no crane swallowing a cork.

But could I contend that I was not a tortoise-shell kitten?

Yukiko's skin was swarthy, giving lie to her name, which meant "snow-child." Below her ample breasts lay the expanse of her midsection, in the middle of which was the well-formed and delicate hollow of her navel. I had lain here, for I "thought it a very fine bed," but I suddenly realized my resting place had now changed itself into a black fedora. The powerful hands of a man in a black suit snatched the black hat away and placed it on his head.

Fantasies of every sort angered and terrified me. I sat at my desk at work waiting for Yukiko's man.

A small, round-shouldered fellow stood by my desk. His garish checkered jacket was so unbecoming it could only have been borrowed. He had the look of a timid man, perhaps a budding artist or a cartoonist come to sell his cartoons.

"Yukiko . . ."

I started when I heard him utter her name. It was a surprise attack, something unexpected.

"Just a minute," I said checking him. He looked around the room.

"Shall we talk in a reception room or somewhere?" he asked diffidently. The company that employed me, however, had leased a small, two-story wood-frame building; the first floor was the business office, the second, the editorial office. There was no space for a reception room.

I invited the man to a nearby coffee shop.

"Quite a surprise, a company with no reception room."

My own surprise was likewise unabated. This thirty-year-old man's hair had thinned considerably, leaving the shape of his head for all to see, and it was certainly unimpressive.

"Don't magazine publishers," he continued, apparently unable to drop the subject, "have steel-frame buildings, the whole thing to themselves?"

"There are magazines like that."

"I can see there's no money here," he said dejectedly. I sensed all the pent-up tension I had been feeling lunge past me harmlessly like an ungainly sumo wrestler. And I felt anger that even this unimpressive man had no choice but to consider *me* unimpressive.

"Listen, friend, you don't have to give up quite so easily, do you?"

As soon as I spoke I realized the absurdity of my words.

The man properly introduced himself at last.

"I'm Masuda."

He took out a folded weekly magazine from the inside pocket of his checkered jacket and set it on the table. It was the weekly we publish.

"I bought it on the way over. It's really awful, isn't it? I didn't have much faith in it as a magazine, but I thought that at least they'd have plenty of money here. Any way you cut it Yukiko has really latched onto a scum-bag."

"And what the hell would you call yourself?"

"I'm scum too. But Yukiko and me are linked by an inseparable bond. Well, anyway, there's no point in two comrades in scum like you and me facing off like this."

He stood up, so I quickly spoke.

"Hey now, wait. You came to shake me down, right? The whole point of a shakedown is that if you think I don't have any money you make me get it any way I can."

My sense of relief that the man—waiting tensely for me to finish—was a weak and feckless *yakuza*, and my exasperation at being held in contempt by such a man, had made me eloquent.

"Listen, friend, if you're scum, you've got to be the baddest scum there is. You slap the belly of a blue-backed fish down on a concrete floor and it splits open, right? Its guts pop out. Above you the summer sun is burning fiercely. The thin membrane around the gut is slimy with fat, and reflects the light of the sun, glistening with all the colors of the rainbow, like machine oil floating on a puddle. That's the sort of shakedown I want to see."

I was drunk with my own words. A brutal surge had thrust itself to the fore.

"Okay then, I'll do the extorting and find some money for you. And I'll give you the money. How much you want? Two hundred thousand or three?"

Masuda seemed to have been listening to me with only half an ear, but now his expression changed. A sly gleam came into his eyes.

"Well, the more the better."

"Fine. Come and see me in a week."

I HAD SOMETHING I could exploit for blackmail. I'd had it for quite a long while, but it never occurred to me to use it. It was a secret in the past of the movie actress Hoshikawa Seiko. Were this secret to become public, there could be no doubt that it would severely damage her popularity.

I called the actress from a phone booth. I was excited, and the idea that I would be a conduit for blackmail money to Masuda goaded me into action. My finger spun the dial eagerly.

I was finally able to get Hoshikawa herself to come to the phone after explaining several times that I wanted to talk to the actress about something very important.

The voice of Hoshikawa Seiko that I had heard in movies and on TV issued from the earpiece.

"What can I do for you?"

I uttered the words at the heart of her secret.

There was a brief moment of silence, then she spoke.

"And what do you want of me?"

Her voice was cloaked in serenity, but I could hear the agitation within.

"I should like to meet you in person," I said, "and talk about this."

"In that case we could meet tonight in the lobby of the Imperial Hotel."

I had once interviewed the actress. That time, too, she had asked to meet in the lobby of the Imperial. I suspect she always told reporters to meet her there. It was good publicity to let people see her being interviewed. She was now making her way from starlet to star. In the circumstances, however, the hotel lobby would have been an inappropriate venue for her.

Don't lose your cool!
I heard her hasten to correct herself.
"No, wait. Come to my home."
She asked me to come at seven o'clock that night. When I got off the suburban train she had told me to take and stepped onto the station platform, I noticed that I was very tense. I told myself this would never do, and recalled the stories of the big-time thieves who, before they would sneak into a house, would empty their bowels by the front gate. As I remembered the stories my tension eased. At which point I suddenly realized I was starving.

There was a stall selling Chinese noodles in front of the station. I ordered a bowl. The middle-aged cook chopped some green onions and dropped them into the steaming bowl.

"Give me lots of onions."

"Hokay! Special service for you!"

He gave me the bowl, a healthy heap of onions on top of the noodles. I bent over the bowl. The steam went up my nostrils and I felt my nose starting to run. I turned my head to the side and blew my nose. This was me at my seediest.

"And Hoshikawa Seiko was pretty much like this in the old days," I muttered to myself. "No, her life was a damn sight worse."

I recalled the time I had met the actress at the Imperial Hotel. A hotel lobby often overwhelms the people in it. It can starkly manifest in them the sense that they do not belong there. That time, however, her presence was one of complete assurance, such that the large chair supporting her body appeared to be in attendance on her. For my part, I had been intimidated, and despised her for telling me to come to the lobby of the Imperial Hotel for the interview. For me it meant remembering something I'd rather forget. I began to lose, little by little, my enthusiasm.

My spirits had revived, however, by the time I left the noodle stall.

"I'll make this woman, graceful as a crane, eat the cork," I told myself as I began walking. But eager to find support for my feelings in a line from a nursery rhyme, I didn't notice then that the outcome was perfectly obvious.

Hoshikawa Seiko was well-matched to her sumptuous sitting room. I sat in a large chair with a thick comforter for the legs. I positioned myself deep in the chair and crossed my legs, but my posture struck me as pretentious and I uncrossed them.

"Let's hear what you have to say."

Her tone was self-assured. I began talking to show that the information I had on her was accurate. Here and there I went into more detail than was necessary. I was intent on attacking her, on hurting her. Her face, however, betrayed no emotion. Apparently, she had long resigned herself to the fact that this day would come and had prepared herself mentally. Her immobile expression infuriated me.

I shifted forward in the chair and leaned toward the actress, whose chair was at a right angle to mine. I tried all the more to hurt her, going into microscopic detail.

She grimaced for an instant, then regained her composure. The whole of her face hadn't contorted. She had knitted her brow and the flares of her nostrils had moved faintly. The instant I saw that movement I thought I caught the pungent smell of onions on my breath. You normally don't notice the smell of what you've eaten, so it may have been my imagination, triggered by the movement of her brow and nostrils. In either case, what *was* certain was that my story caused no change in her expression. Reflexively, I sat far back in the chair, my thoughts sour and my gaze on the flares of Hoshikawa Seiko's nose.

What's wrong with having some noodles? You're well off now, but there was a time when you couldn't even afford a single bowl.

Her nose, however, was delicately sculpted, conspicuous by its beauty of line. It was elegant, like a subtly crafted *objet*

— 111 —

d'art, and there it was before me proving itself unsuited to inhaling a tepid breath reeking of onions.

"And just what are you going to do?" she asked me when I had finished talking.

"I intend to publish it in our magazine."

"You can't do that."

"Just because you tell me I can't . . ."

"Surely you can see there's no point in picking on a helpless woman," she said, but her tone lacked any hint of entreaty.

"You're not a helpless woman."

She gave me a searching look.

"Aren't you embarrassed to be doing such a thing?"

"You can't do the work I do if you get embarrassed."

I had delivered an honest-to-God tough guy line, but it was obvious to me it had no force. I had even lost my obsession that I cover her with ignominy. My efforts now were half-hearted, my energy gone. Our conversation proceeded under its own momentum.

"You're determined to publish it?"

"I am."

"There's no way I can get you not to?"

"I wouldn't say that."

"Money?"

"Right."

"You're saying I need only buy this material you have, right? But no matter how much I buy from you, there'll be no end to it, since it's all there in your head."

I didn't respond.

"I want you to promise me. You will cause me absolutely no more trouble about this matter after I buy the material from you."

"I promise."

"You really do?"

"Yes."

She leaned forward from her chair, bent down, and retrieved a small tape recorder from under the table. Her slender, beautiful finger hit the rewind button. The two reels whirred and stopped, then began turning slowly in the opposite direction.

My voice boomed out of the device, a sound vile to my ears. The stench of onion clung to each word.

"I promise."

"You really do?"

"Yes."

The machine repeated our entire conversation. She turned it off.

"Now listen to me. If you break your promise, I'll have you charged with blackmail. This tape is my witness."

Suddenly, her expression was one of mockery.

"Oh, I just remembered. You haven't yet decided how much money you want, have you."

She had the self-possession of someone who had all the cards. She studied me, her look amply guarded. Her mind moved quickly and focused itself on the amount that would momentarily issue from my mouth. A hardness suffused Hoshikawa Seiko's face.

"Twenty thousand yen."

In the situation I was in, setting the amount lower than she had anticipated was the only thing I could do. Seeing this hardness in her face, I essayed a figure, and my calculation was on the mark.

"Twenty thousand yen? That will satisfy you, won't it."

Her voice was buoyant now. A suggestion of coarseness heretofore unheard crept into her voice and animated her face, where the actress's secret past traced itself like invisible ink over a flame.

"That's fine."

Not here the image of the sun fiercely burning over fish guts slapped down on concrete. I'm wriggling cheerlessly on an ashen surface. And Hoshikawa Seiko and Yukiko and her unimpressive boyfriend are likewise wriggling on the same surface.

YUKIKO VISITED ME IN my room.

"Masuda came to see me the other day," I told her.

"So he told me."

"You knew about it, didn't you."

"Yeah."

"He wasn't what I expected," I essayed. "He's not the menacing type at all."

Yukiko looked me full in the face: "I'm not so sure about that."

"I didn't give him any money."

"That's what he told me. He said there was no way he was going to get anything from someone like you."

I felt I'd stuck my foot right into a trap. I really didn't know why. Lost in thought, I was silent for a while. I wondered if I were the kitten napping inside the hat.

"You afraid of him?"

"What can I say?" she answered unhelpfully. "Anyway, it doesn't matter, does it?"

She began slowly to take off her clothes. I glimpsed the sole of her foot as she took off a stocking. I was sure I saw a red, swollen welt there, a new one. This was in spite of the fact that there no longer should have been any need for him to pump her about me. I didn't say a word, however. For it occurred to me that this welt was perhaps something that Masuda and Yukiko, the two of them, needed.

"Did Masuda tell you to come here?"

"What can I say?" she answered, as vague as before.

"Did you get any money?" she suddenly asked.

She knew that I had tried to shake someone down, so I realized that's what she was asking me about.

"Did Masuda send you over to ask?"

"No! You didn't get any money, did you?"

— 114 —

"No, I didn't," I lied. It was not, however, a complete lie. You could say that it pretty much amounted to not getting any money.

"Masuda told me you weren't likely to."

I had thought Masuda's eyes had gleamed with slyness, but I suspected now it might have been the gleam of appraisal.

"Why did you come here?"

Yukiko approached me, her bare arms outstretched. "What does it matter?"

A deep furrow etched itself between her eyebrows, but I caught no scent from her skin. Her body was clearly damp with sweat, nonetheless.

"They finished their experiments at the lab?"

"Why?"

"I don't smell them anymore."

I saw a faint smile cross her lips, and suddenly I understood.

"You've moved, haven't you."

"I sure have. I moved in with Masuda. We've decided to live together."

A trace of the vertical furrow remained between Yukiko's eyebrows. She would take this mark back to the room where Masuda was waiting. For Masuda—and for Yukiko as well—these furrows raised by another man were perhaps indispensable. I could not be sure, but that might have been exactly how it was.

Yukiko was dressed now.

"I'll be back, okay?" she said as she left.

I spent the twenty thousand yen on myself. I spent it eating good food I hadn't had in a long while and buying cheap whores. I spent it sparingly, so sparingly.

THREE DREAMS

夢三つ

TRANSLATED BY LAWRENCE ROGERS

· 1 ·

"I wish I knew whose face it is."

Hoshie was talking, and it was her co-worker Yukari who was doing the listening. The bar girls were in the changing room and work was about to begin.

"What sort of face? A face you've seen before or one you've never ever seen?"

"I'm not sure. The surprising thing is it's a face I'm very familiar with, and when I see it I'll probably recognize it, 'Oh yeah, that's so-and-so.'"

"Stop it!" shouted Keiko hysterically. She was touching up her lipstick as she looked at her face in her compact mirror. "You're talking about your fantasies again! It's all you ever do! It gets on my nerves!"

And in fact a deep furrow etched itself between her eyebrows.

"You call them fantasies, Keiko, but I'm talking about a real dream."

"They're the same thing. It's idiotic!"

For Keiko, who was, heart and soul, a bar girl, and the possessor of an exceedingly realistic turn of mind, their conversation about a dream was irritating in the extreme.

Hoshie and Yukari exchanged glances and said nothing.

What form had the face taken in her dream?

Hoshie was living in a room that had no floor. She had a vanity table and a chest and other household effects. If she had no floorboards, you would expect that her furniture and she herself would be floating in space; that part defies reason.

This lack offered no particular hindrance to the daily routine in her room, yet Hoshie was obsessed.

I really hate not having a floor. It's really no good living in a room that has no floor.

When she would direct her gaze below where she was sitting, she would see that a black void lay open before her and the damp smell of earth seemed to rise up to her.

"It's so depressing," she muttered, standing up and walking over to the vanity. Her image reflected in the mirror, she applied a thick layer of lipstick. Then she returned to where she had been and sat down. After she had done that, she suddenly spoke out loud.

"Oh dear!"

I have no flooring, but I'm still able to move about.

Once that was in Hoshie's mind, it was as though she were tied to the spot where she sat. Should she absentmindedly move, she could easily fall into the black hole. She drew back and remained absolutely still. The space where she could sit became ever narrower. A flood of water was all around her, and she was sitting atop the roof. The water was gradually rising.

She wondered if someone would come to her rescue, but did not expect that to happen. Hoshie lived in the room by herself.

The door opened. A man came in.

"Hey, I'm back."

She couldn't tell who it was. He had four or five long boards under one arm and carried a saw in his other hand.

Hoshie saw what he had under his arm.

Ah, I can get him to lay down my floor for me.

She tried to look at his face. Who is this guy? She heard a man's voice.

"Whoa! What're you sitting on?"

The voice made her shudder. As her body moved it seemed to her that she was about to fall into the black hole. She crouched down, yet there should have been nothing to support her.

The moment she realized this Hoshie's body began to drop. She didn't have the sensation that she was tumbling into the hole, rather that she was slowly descending like some mechanical contraption.

Just before the inside of the room disappeared from sight, Hoshie was sure she got a look at the man's face, and yet. . . .

· 2 ·

Every time one of the regulars entered the bar and sat down Hoshie made it a point to look at his face.

"I had a weird dream," she would say, hoping to provoke his interest, but no man seemed willing to hear her out. One man was blunt.

"Nothing's as pointless as talk about one's dreams or love life."

"How come?"

"Usually the only person who finds it interesting is the person who had the dream."

Hoshie looked at each of the men.

He's not the guy.

She was superimposing the face of the man in front of her on the indistinct face of the man in her dreams.

A middle-aged man named Tada entered. Hoshie had gone out to eat with him several times. After the meal he had seen her home, but they had no relationship beyond that, yet she felt close to him. Hoshie was comfortable with Tada for some reason.

"I have all these weird dreams."

"Really?"

Tada's tone suggested he wasn't particularly interested either. Yukari, nearby, jumped in.

"C'mon, Tada, listen to what she has to say. They're really strange dreams."

"Really? Hearing about someone's dreams, by and large, is pretty boring."

"It's about a missing person," Yukari told him.

"A missing person?"

"Which is to say, it goes like this," Yukari began, taking over from Hoshie. When she was finished Tada stared at Hoshie.

"It's interesting that you live in a room with no floor."

"Isn't it," Yukari said, emphasizing the point.

"And the problem is the guy."

"No problem there."

"And why not?"

"It's me," Tada said.

"How can that be?" Hoshie asked.

"You had that dream the day before yesterday, right?"

"Right, the day before yesterday."

"I remember carrying lumber for flooring under my left arm, holding a saw in my right hand, and going into your dream the night before last."

"You're kidding me!"

"If you think I'm kidding, I'll go home with you tonight. I'll put down your flooring and do a good job of it."

"That's not funny."

"If you're looking for the guy from among the men who come here, then that's more or less how it'll be."

"I wonder if you might be right."

"That's how it is," Tada said, once again looking at Hoshie. "But you're a strange woman, you know. Being able to have a dream like that is a gift. And yet in the world you're living in now your gift doesn't seem to get put to use all that much, does it."

· 3 ·

That night Hoshie had an unpleasant dream.

She walked into a large, weathered old house. The building seemed to be a lecture hall, one with a very high ceiling.

The desks were lined up neatly, row upon row, and each had a number written on it in white paint.

Hoshie had a slip of paper in her hand on which was written a large numeral. The slip was apparently an admission ticket for an examination, and the exam was about to begin.

The number on Hoshie's exam ticket was "1." The lights were on in the hall, but the lighting was yellow and dim. She walked about looking for her desk.

Desks with the numbers "2," "3," "4," and "5" written in white paint were lined up in a neat row, but Hoshie's number "1" was nowhere to be seen. And the desks were filling up one after the other. All sorts of men and women, young and old, found their desks, sat down, and waited, facing straight ahead. They were probably waiting for the examinations to be handed out, yet it wasn't clear what the exam was for.

Hoshie simply knew, however, that she could find herself in trouble if she didn't take the exam. Her fretfulness grew more intense, but she still could not find her desk.

A thought suddenly occurred to her: perhaps her seat was outside the lecture hall. She left the building, walking briskly.

Outdoors night had fallen.

Outdoors there was a festival.

Drums sounded incessantly, and Hoshie was instantly engulfed by the throng. Shoulders bumped against shoulders, flanks rubbed against flanks, and on both sides of Hoshie, who was jostled about as she moved along, there stood night stalls, their lights shining brightly.

The colors of the chemical "magic flowers" in bloom under water and traditional Kintarō candies in the night stalls leapt fitfully into view between one head and another, one shoulder and another.

At last she came to the end of the stalls. The merrymaking had been transformed; it was now on an expansive plain. Young men wearing twisted headbands sat in a circle carousing.

Hoshie stopped nearby and called out to them.

"Uh, could you tell me where I am?"

When she opened her hand she saw the slip of paper, damp with sweat. Written on it was the number "1."

One of the young men stood up, left the circle and came over to Hoshie.

Looking at her palm, he spoke casually.

"Where? This is a funeral home, one just built."

The youth's breath smelled faintly of saké. His extended finger pointed into the darkness.

"It's over there," he said.

Hoshie began walking in the direction he was pointing. The tree-lined road went on and on. She walked along wondering why she had to walk toward a funeral home.

Suddenly she sensed a strangeness inside her nose, and in the next instant something slipped out of both nostrils. Looking down at the end of her nose, she saw narrow white strips.

She touched them with the tips of her fingers. They had the feel of thin paper. The long strips of white paper hung from each nostril. She took hold of them with her thumb and forefinger and pulled, but there was no break in the paper, which kept coming. No matter how much she drew out, it kept coming, almost gushing out of her nose.

As she continued to draw the paper out she rushed ahead, taking short mincing steps.

"Ah, ah, ah," she said, making a deep guttural sound as she continued to run on through the night; then she woke up.

Three Dreams

· 4 ·

Hoshie had another unpleasant dream the next night.

She was walking along a road at night. There was farmland on either side of the road and no sign of people. There were no street lights, of course, and she saw no moon or stars in the sky, yet it was not pitch black. A pale purple light bathed everything.

Suddenly a dark figure appeared in a field near Hoshie. It looked terribly stooped, but she realized that was because it was carrying a cloth-wrapped bundle on its back.

The man set his bundle down on the ground and looked all about, his back still bent.

Hoshie was standing close by, yet it appeared that he had not noticed her. When he had finished carefully checking the area and making sure there was no one about, he began digging.

Using his hands as shovels, he had dug a deep hole in almost no time. The man put the bundle into the hole, covered it with earth and carefully smoothed out the soil.

He once again looked around, then disappeared into thin air.

Hoshie walked into the field. The earth where the man had buried the bundle was a different color, so she could tell where it was right away.

I wonder what he buried.

She heard a faint sound. It was a clear yet faint sound that occurred at precise, fixed intervals: tick-tock, tick-tock. It was the sound a device of some sort would make.

Hoshie wondered if he had buried an alarm clock, and at that instant the earth exploded before her eyes. There was a thunderous roar, and clumps of dirt flew through the air in a shower of sparks, but these were multicolored and caused in Hoshie little sense of danger. It was an explosion that somehow provided her a margin of safety, as though fire had got to a bundle of sparklers in a night stall.

When the smoke cleared a bit Hoshie saw a tree standing in front of her, a slender tree twice her height. It had, however, huge leaves ill-suited to such a thin trunk, leaves so lush that they overlapped one another; fruit peeked out from amongst them.

"I wonder what kind of fruit this is."

She took several steps toward the tree and looked up from under the branches that spread over her like an umbrella. Five large pieces of fruit hung in a row, each hard against the other.

Hoshie screamed in spite of herself.

The five pieces were human heads. They were the face of a man; all five had the same man's face. They had the same face, and yet you could say the faces were different. That was because each of the five faces was slightly deformed in its own way: a face with contorted lips, a face with a blinded eye, one with the bridge of the nose missing. Not one of them was whole.

The five faces were all expressionless, but their gaze was directed at Hoshie. Whose face was it? She could not remember ever having seen it. They were expressionless, yet the deformed parts served to function as expressions; the five faces swayed back and forth, jostling one another.

Hoshie was awakened by her own screams.

She had been sweating lightly, yet her bed was cold. The part of the bed beneath her body was also cold, as though she had no body temperature. It would be a nuisance to go to work. If she didn't, however, her livelihood would immediately be in jeopardy.

I wonder if I'm coming down with something.

Twins

双生

Translated by Lawrence Rogers

· 1 ·

He could hear the sound of singing coming from the next room. Women's voices were blending in song, one above the other. Etō stretched his body out in bed, but a heavy drowsiness still held him.

He opened his eyes only slightly. Judging from the light in the room he guessed it was close to noon. It was Sunday, so after reassuring himself anew that he would not be expected to go to the office, he closed his eyes.

The door dividing the two rooms opened slightly and the face of his wife Saeko peered in.

"Dear, Utako's come to see us."

"I'm aware of that."

"How about getting up."

"I hear you."

"Dear."

"In five minutes."

He pulled the quilt up over his head.

Once again he heard the voices singing. The voices of women were nicely harmonizing, Saeko taking the treble and Utako the lower register. When they were children the sisters had sung children's songs on the radio. What they were singing now was also a child's song, adult voices singing a child's song.

He tried once again to go back to sleep, but his sleepiness was beginning to fade as the words of the song came to him, one by one, under the quilt.

> *... the dark, long flight of stairs*
> *I know there's nothing unusual,*
> *but sometimes I wonder*
> *if something's not following me and I look back.*
> *When I pass a dark corner*
> *I always stare hard at it,*
> *but I'm ever so grateful*
> *I've a candle in my hand.*

An image presented itself willy-nilly to his brain under the quilt. The scene might seem to have been evoked precisely by the lyrics of the song, but that was not the case. An image from his childhood had been intruding into his thoughts from time to time.

WHEN HE WAS A child they would finish the evening meal in the living room, then, a little while later, he would have to go by himself to a bedroom on the second floor. The living room *shōji* opened onto a long hallway. The hallway led to a gray wall, then went on in a ninety-degree turn to the left, at the end of which was a flight of stairs.

On the right-hand side of the hallway where you turned left was a door that led to the garden. That door was always open, so when you turned in that direction you found yourself facing a large rectangle of empty space.

The long hallway was a good place to play in the daytime. He would play marbles and run his toy cars there. The dimness of the hall didn't bother him. The space that opened to the garden was drenched in the bright light of the sun. The trees in the garden, a radiant green glow, seemed to almost burst through their rectangular frame.

This very same doorway was utterly transformed when night fell. Standing open partway down the long hallway, it became a black hole.

"The hall's scary," he complained.

"Light a candle and take it with you," a grown-up told him. "There're candles on the family altar."

But he was afraid to walk along with a candle. If he had a candle he would want to lift it up and peer into the black hole. He didn't believe he would then see the earth and the trees of the garden in the light of the candle. To his eyes the black hole was the entryway to a different world.

He would walk down the hall, eyes straight ahead, and come to the wall at the end. To his right was that black yawning. Hurrying, he would turn left. In that instant he would sense a bright light flaring flame-like in the corner of his eye. He sensed the black hole was illuminated by a blinding light at its center. Yet he had no desire to turn his head and gaze at it. He was afraid to look.

Etō had been married to Saeko for three years. He married her four years after graduating from college with honors and having been hired by a company of the first rank. He was a handsome young man with an imposing physical presence. His facial expressions were a bit lacking in nuance, but this rather made him appear dependable and as someone marked for success. He had the ability to look good in anything and would not flinch at even a silk hat and tails. At his firm he was someone who was noticed, a future executive. And Etō himself had his eye on the present and the future. He did not look back at the past.

This had changed, however, about a month before.

He finally got out of bed. He pulled on his pants, put on a sweater, and looked into the next room. Two faces simultaneously turned. Two identical faces were looking at him.

Saeko had been born first, so Utako was the "younger sister;" the two were, nonetheless, twins. Utako was not married, so her clothes were naturally more in fashion, yet their faces were so alike you couldn't tell them apart.

"You two look more alike than ever, don't you," he said almost reproachfully as he compared the two faces.

The two women exchanged glances but said nothing. Behind the two faces was a television screen on which, side by side, were the faces of twin singers.

"Those singers don't look as much alike as they used to," Etō said. "They were perfect doubles before. You agree?"

"You're right," the twins answered in unison.

"That's because," he began, "any change in a woman's face is due to her man. You can bet that they each have a lover. So that's why they look different now. Am I right?"

"You're right."

"That being the case, how come you two still look alike?"

"Hey, we're a special case."

"Special?"

"We've been alike in everything from day one, you name it. We're not going to change an eyelash."

"Utako," he said, turning to the face that was identical to Saeko's, "do you have a lover?"

"Hmm, how should I answer that?"

"If he looks anything like me, then my logic holds, eh?"

Utako laughed but said nothing.

The twin vocalists on the TV screen began singing a children's song. This was unusual, since they normally sang jazz tunes. As soon as he noticed this he ventured another question.

"The song a minute ago, was that coming from the TV?"

"The song a minute ago? The nursery rhyme? We were singing it."

Etō was silent.

TWINS

"Hurry and go wash up," Saeko said as she reached out and turned off the television. "Then we'll eat."

The women's harmonizing, one voice above the other, reached him clear and loud as he was brushing his teeth in the lavatory. The melody was the same as the one he had heard in bed, but the lyrics were different.

I'm a strong boy in the daytime
Not a thing makes me 'fraid.
I play war and pretend to hunt.
I even kill big lizards,
but when it gets dark
it's somehow all creepy.
I'm unhappy if I've no candlelight
when I go off to bed.

· 2 ·

It's night and Saeko's face is directly below Etō's, one body atop the other. Saeko's brows are knitted, and gradually her features contort. Looking at her face, a thought abruptly comes to him: *Isn't this Utako?*

A month before Murai, a co-worker at the office, had put something in his ear.

"I happened to see your wife yesterday. She was with a young American."

"Where?"

"In a place not entirely proper."

"Which means you were also in such a place."

"I was just passing by."

Etō studied his coworker's face. It might be said of the man that he had a habit of talking nonsense and taking pleasure in seeing his listener's disquiet.

"I suspect you're lying."

"I'm not lying, but maybe I didn't see what I thought I saw."

Etō said nothing.

"Such a thing is impossible, is it?"

"Impossible, I'd say."

"If that's the case, then I'm doubtless mistaken," Murai said, falling silent. A little later he spoke again.

"Women are really scary. I'm talking about my own situation. I'm having a hell of a time with Yuriko."

Etō knew the name, a name from the tiresome accounts of Murai's love life. He boasted that she was the ideal mistress. They had been seeing each other for the last five years, and she had accepted the situation, he said. That is, they would only sleep together, not marry. Not once had she displayed a troublesome attitude.

"She wants to get married?"

"Were that the case the hellishness would be a great deal less."

Over those five years Murai was sure he had learned everything there was to learn about Yuriko. Or rather, while he didn't smugly presume that he understood her to the innermost recesses of her soul, at the very least he believed he knew every square inch of her body. And he was also sure of her anguished expression of ecstasy. However, one night, that expression on her face, she let something slip.

Murai said that with her eyes half-closed—their expression suggesting that she suddenly realized the face before her was Murai's—she spoke in disjointed fragments, the gist of which was that if it were Murai with her she couldn't let herself feel more satisfaction than this.

"Five years is quite a long time. And yet there are still sides of Yuriko I'm unaware of, and there's a man who sees those other sides."

"Is that really what it is?"

"That's what it is. Let me be clear about this. I'm not saying I'm surprised there's another man. I detected signs of that earlier."

"Yet isn't that the result of trying to make her live within the limits you forced on her?"

"But it doesn't mean I could put my mind at ease if we married. When you marry there's often the tendency, among other things, to delude yourself that you know your spouse's heart inside and out."

The conversation returned to its starting point. Murai now believed the woman with the young American was, after all, Etō's wife.

"There's a chance that what you saw was my wife's sister."

He had said it without really intending to.

"Her sister? They look alike?"

"You can say that. They're twins."

"There's a twin sister? You were keeping that to yourself, eh?"

"I wasn't keeping it to myself. But neither do I go out of my way to tell people."

"You were keeping it to yourself, as I'd expect. You find that when it comes to twins. They'll either hide the fact or, conversely, dress up identically and walk around, two peas in a pod. It's one or the other."

Etō was sure that the sisters were always together when he first got to know Saeko. Even in the case of twins there are pairs who look less alike than ordinary sisters. And though their features might be alike, some pairs give the clear impression that they're different as night and day. It was close to impossible to tell Saeko and Utako apart, however. Their clothes had been absolutely identical. And they rather took pride in this sameness. Etō did not have the feeling that they had sunny dispositions because they had discarded the common Japanese fixation about twins. He didn't sense that sort of distortion.

The two women would confront Etō, bringing their utterly identical faces together, pressing cheek against cheek: "Which one of us is Saeko? Try and guess!"

Or they would declare together, "We're the same inside, too."

The flagrance of their words excited Etō, but the import of what they said simply was that, from their thinking to their interests and tastes, they were similar.

To give an example, Utako used to stay over at a friend's house on Saturday nights. Saeko decided one Sunday afternoon to see a movie and entered a theater in town. You select a seat when you go to the movies based on your own preferences. Saeko sat fifteen rows back and a bit to the left. When she happened to look to see who was sitting immediately to her left, there was Utako. This, of course, was not something they had agreed on beforehand. How they would spend Sunday afternoon, the choice of movie each wanted to see, their selection of a seat, these were all in agreement, so they both ended up in the same movie house at the same time.

That being the case, how was it that he had chosen Saeko? Would Utako have been a poor choice for him? You couldn't have expected Etō to tell the difference if Utako had turned up for the date at the agreed-upon location in her sister's place. No, there is no guarantee that that sort of thing hadn't happened earlier. It may well be that within the sisters, flaunting their identical faces and pressing cheek against cheek, there lay concealed a mentality unlike that of the average person.

If, in the theater that is the world we live in, the seat chosen by Saeko was Etō, we should not be surprised if Utako were to attempt to sit in that same seat.

The single drop of poison that Murai had dropped into Etō's heart a month earlier was gradually spreading and growing.

Could it be Utako?

Etō, looking at the face immediately beneath him and suddenly assailed by that doubt, was flustered by the thought; in spite of himself he called out the name in her ear: "Utako."

Saeko's eyes opened wide. She showed no sign she was offended, however. On the contrary, her tone was gentle.

"I'm Saeko. You want to make love to Utako?

"It's not that."

"Making love to me is making love to Utako. We're exactly the same."

"You say you're the same, but how can you know that?"

She said nothing.

"The thought suddenly came to me just now that the woman with me might be Utako, not you. It's the first time I've thought such a thing."

Saeko still held Etō in her wide-eyed gaze. She showed no fear at his words, nor had they taken her by surprise. Her eyes signaled gentle acceptance.

"You've been married to me for three years. How is it that you two remain identical?

"Utako apparently has a lover."

"An American?"

"Oh my! How do you know that?"

"Why are you two the same . . . in spite of that fact? Are you conspiring together so that you won't change?"

Saeko, saying not a word, wrapped her arms around his neck, pulled his face to hers, and covered his lips with hers.

· 3 ·

When I get into my little bed
I pull the quilt over my head
and I'm ever so secretly peeking
at the shadows toward me creeping.
The shadows reach the corner of the room
and cover everything in gloom,
But I feel no fright.
for 'tis fun to watch my little candle's light.

The next Sunday Etō, sleeping lightly, could hear singing. It was the voices of women joined in song, one above the other.

"This candle is useless," Etō mumbled, then quickly realized the two voices were not singing in harmony. They were singing the same tune in unison, which came to his ear almost as one voice.

The singing sounded to him as though Saeko and Utako were conspiring to tempt him. To where did they intend to tempt him? Saeko and Utako had constructed a world of their own. It was a world where the rules were completely unlike those of the world Etō inhabited. They were trying to tempt him into that world. That's what it sounded like to him.

The two women continued to sing.

I'm a strong boy in the daytime
Not a thing makes me 'fraid.
I play war and pretend to hunt.
I even kill big lizards,

Etō, however, was not strong, even in the daytime now. For the last month his standing as an able company employee had been coming unraveled little by little. And at the same time something of a shadow had fallen over his good looks.

The singing ceased.

The door opened slightly.

Two identical voices came into the room.

"How about getting up?"

Two utterly identical faces, one above the other, peered at him through the opening.

A Certain Married Couple

ある夫婦

Translated by William Matsuda

· 1 ·

I went out, putting on shoes that had been worn down at the heels and fixed; metal plates had been tacked on to make the repair. It's not a particularly unusual way to fix shoes, but they are prone to slipping. It's no problem if I'm walking on dirt, but on pavement I slip. I slipped quite a bit, even on the platform in Tokyo Station, and by the time I left through the Yaesu ticket gate I was having trouble walking. I lifted my feet, soles level with the ground, and lowered them the same way, my back hunched over. Just as I was recalling that I looked like this when I went to the hospital with a bubo, a swollen lymph gland in the groin, my eyes met those of a middle-aged man walking briskly toward me.

"Hi!" he said.

"Hi, Choku!"

His name was Naokichi, but everyone called him Choku.

"Where're you headed?" he asked, looking very much the gentleman in his suit and tie.

"Where am I headed, you ask? I can't walk for slipping."

"Slipping? You mean your shoes?"

"Yeah, my shoes. So let's have some tea somewhere. Haven't seen you for a long while, am I right?"

"You are. Let's do that."

· 2 ·

When we finally walked out of the station complex the city was still bathed in the light of morning. I had come to pick up some medicine from a gastrointestinal clinic.

We sat across from each other in a coffee shop.

"Miss!" Choku called out to the waitress, "two coffees, please."

He then turned to me: "I don't suppose this is a good time for whiskey."

"All things considered, neither of us ought to be up and about this time of day."

"You're right there, taking us for the nocturnal animals we are!" Choku said with a grin. Three front teeth, which should have been missing, peered out at me in perfect alignment.

"Hey, you got your teeth fixed!"

"Business has been good, and women still find me attractive, so why not?" Choku said, keeping one step ahead of me.

"You're still retired from the business, right?"

"Well, I'm retired, but I still have some ties."

"The business" referred to the world of those who make their living introducing women to men. In other words, Choku used to be a pimp. Now he seemed to put food on the table by writing one thing and another, but only *seemed* to. Nonetheless, I was not going to pursue the matter further. Since Choku was a university graduate, however, making a living this way was not the least bit unusual.

I've known Choku for well over ten years, but I've never used his good offices myself to get a woman. Instead, I get him to tell me all sorts of stories.

Laymen such as myself tend to pronounce the Japanese word for pimp *ponbiki*, but Choku told me that in the trade it's pronounced *ponhiki*. Since they tap (*pon*) the shoulder and pull (*hiki*) at the sleeves of men passing by, they are called *ponhiki*. Choku also tells me that there's a yin and a yang in drawing in clients off the street.[1]

Tapping a passerby's shoulder, opening the palm of your hand and saying boldly "Hey mister, we got some nice girls here" is yang. However, turning up the palm you used to tap his shoulder, curling your fingers in and moving your index and middle fingers to lure him while you whisper with an air of secrecy into his ear "Hey mister, we got some nice girls here" is yin.

Choku started standing out on the street shortly after the war ended, but it took quite a bit of time before he was able to call out to passersby. Since he was a college-educated intellectual, it took him twice as long as it would have anyone else. Choku often used to say, "My earnings rank forty-fifth or forty-sixth in Japan. I'm a terrible pimp."

As we sat across from each other in the coffee shop and drank our coffee, I ventured a few questions.

"Number one in Japan is still Hanegi, right?"

"There's no change there."

"Number two is Hiro Boy?"

"The same goes for him. Number one is Hanegi, number two is Hiro Boy. There is no number three or four."

"What about number five?"

"They're fighting over that spot right now."

As for a bigwig like Hanegi, the story is that he used to handle a certain actress many years ago. She's so famous you'd be surprised if you heard her name; she enjoyed quite a bit of fame even then. Of course, not any man would do as a partner. You see, Hanegi carefully selected her clients and recommended them to her. The word pimp does not suit circumstances such as these. Perhaps we should say he is a call girl manager.

---

1 In traditional Chinese cosmology yin and yang are complementary opposites. Yin refers to the passive, dark principle while yang refers to the active, bright principle.

Several years ago I wrote something called *Call Girl*, and as part of my research I had Choku introduce me to all sorts of people. Among them was Kuroi, a manager of call girls. He was a middle-aged man with a round, plump face who wore horn-rimmed glasses and came across as a good-natured fellow. His wife was a shrewd-looking young woman who talked a lot and wore fancy glasses. Their work, which they did as a couple, was managing call girls.

Their business, ostensibly, was that of a plant rental service for coffee shops, cabarets, and the like. When you pushed open the door of a coffee shop there would be a potted windmill palm, for example, and a month later the pot would have a different plant in it. It was that sort of potted-plant leasing.

I went to the rental plant office, a single room, where I was made a member. Not a member eligible for plant leasing, but for woman leasing. When you became a member they gave you a booklet of ten coupons.

The Kurois were a cheerful couple, and showed me some scurrilous photos taken overseas. There was one picture that was strange. In the front there was no hair, but it was bushy in the back and looked like a tail. At the time I gazed at the photo with great interest, but now I wonder if it was just a fake.

Speaking of which, those membership coupons were not what they seemed. They expired before I could use even half of them. The story behind that is . . . well, rather than go into that and to keep things simple, let's just say the coupons all expired at once.

One morning when I was glancing over the newspaper I noticed the photos of two familiar faces, a man and a woman, side by side on the local news page. It was the Kuroi couple. According to the article, they had been running a con game involving electrical appliances. It also noted an additional crime, related to call girls, had been uncovered. It was explained that the con game came to light after the two had a falling-out, which is to say, the wife had conspired with her lover and plotted to murder her husband by poisoning him, but they were not successful.

Choku still apologizes.

"I'm sorry for putting you through so much trouble with that."

Then he always adds, "I warned you to be careful, but you went and bought those damned coupons."

"By the way," I asked, "whatever happened to that couple?"

"Well, they got out of prison. Then they got back together."

"They're back together, you say? But didn't she try to poison him?"

"That's what happened, but now they're getting along fine."

Try as I might, I cannot comprehend their situation.

· 3 ·

Now, on to Hiro Boy, the number two pimp in all Japan. Since my original intent in taking up my pen was to write about Hiro Boy, what I have written thus far seems like a long prologue. As might be expected, Hiro Boy was someone I had Choku introduce me to when I was doing my research. He was a small man in his thirties who looked thin, but he had a wiry, tough physique one had best respect. We agreed to meet at a coffee shop in Shimbashi, then chatted as I took him around to two or three bars. In the car that took us from bar to bar Hiro Boy suddenly said something to himself. Although he was talking to himself, he spoke so that I could hear him, and it struck me as out of the blue, considering the banality of the conversation up to that point.

"I get it! Because I've been reading this guy's stuff. I get that he don't get it."

These were words that I could not let pass. Of course, he was criticizing my writing on call girls, but having these comments come from the person right next to me made them all the more shocking.

"What is it I don't get?" I asked in response. Not looking for an argument, I just wanted him to show me where I'd got it wrong.

Hiro Boy said, however, "He don't get it."

I asked him to be more specific, but he just repeated himself. I'd heard that this Hiro Boy faithfully kept a diary, and depending on how things went, I was thinking of asking him to let me read it. Under the circumstances, however, it didn't seem to be in the cards. Most unfortunate, I thought.

I have some knowledge of the world of call girls, but ultimately I'm an outsider. As far as the red-light districts go, I believe I've accumulated a fair amount of knowledge, but in the final analysis I'm merely someone passing through their world.

Since I was aware of my limitations, I found Hiro Boy's comment painful.

"A story I read on call girls not too long ago was good," Hiro Boy said, dodging my question. Since he came out with that, it was that much harder for me to remain unperturbed.

"Who wrote the story?"

"Hmm, who was it?"

"Was it a translation?"

"No, it was Japanese."

Unable to recall the author's name, Hiro Boy started to give me the plot. I listened carefully, figuring that if I learned what literary work had impressed him, I might have a clue to his dissatisfaction with me.

However, as his recounting progressed my disappointment grew. The story of unknown authorship was clearly a commonplace melodrama. The call girl and her man, who acted as her pimp, were tragic heroes, up to their necks in sentimentality.

What? That's it?

That was my gut reaction, but I did not say as much. Hiro Boy's statement that I didn't get it meant, "He don't get the sadness that cuts into our wretched bodies." So my asking him to be more specific doubtless only left him incapable of giving me a real answer.

I began to feel I had an idea as to the contents of Hiro Boy's diary.

Meeting with Hiro Boy was now pointless. That being the case, I decided I would place my hopes in Hiro Boy's actual abilities as a *ponbiki*.

· 4 ·

There is also the issue of whether or not people who live in one world know more about their own world than the people who are just passing through. For example, women writers are grouped together as females from the time they are born. However, it does not follow that the "women" these people depict provide us with more reality than the "women" that men, who always write from the outside, depict.

I had hoped for Hiro Boy's eyes to be unclouded by emotion. I had hoped for two all-seeing eyeballs free and easy right in the middle of the call girl's world.

I once bought seven notebooks called "Diary of a Prostitute" from a male prostitute, a beauty in drag who had had an operation, someone you were unlikely to recognize was a man.

"Listen, when I was in high school," she said, "I chaired the literary club."

For an instant I erroneously imagined a girls' high school, but at the time, of course, she was chairing as a male.

So I had hopes for her special take, but in her diary I found only a string of sentimental snippets.

The following are examples.

> You are everything, you who goes tooth and nail for me. Relax and have a cigarette. Yet Akiko, no, it permeates all of Akiko like air. Your pain. As for going on living, as for this life of twisted love, I shall show you, as over and over again I pile up sand in heaps, even though it gives way each time.

These days I wake up awfully early. It could be because of the stupor from the medicine or because the factory next door is so noisy. Days when midsummer presses upon me I get up and see how it will go, and within a turquoise curtain the apartment falls quiet as the grave, and being in the room is like being under water. Summer, the recollections of summer last year, appalling, but nonetheless the past after all, and nostalgia curiously tinged with sorrow comes to oppress me. Summer is hell when you're addicted to drugs. You break into a sweat, which quickly runs off you.

Or dispirited impressions like the following. (What I wanted were details of how, when her back was against the wall of life, only a few drops of sweat ran off her.)

This woman Kelly, just what sort of woman is she? A woman in love with love. Her thinking sometime is child-like, depending on how you look at it. But when it comes to work she's an adult. She's so matter-of-fact it scares me, but she dreams of loving like a conventional woman. Cross-purposes. I'm puzzled. Unlike her, I no longer dream of finding love. For me there was no real love. Finding it is difficult and I'd guess a lot of people pass it by unaware. To me love is something that belongs to the distant past. When I was in middle and high school I pined out of love, my breast near-constricted when the sun went down. The fact that I can no longer love is for me supremely depressing.

· 5 ·

That night I developed a relationship with Hiro Boy for the first time that was essentially customer-pimp. He took me to the bars that he frequented and paid for drinks. Then we set off in his car, him driving.

Hiro Boy stopped the car at the entrance to a narrow street and disappeared. After a while he came back with a woman in tow. The plan was that I would look her over. We made the rounds of several places, but none of the women interested me. It wasn't that my tastes were so demanding, but, strangely enough, none of the women I saw that night interested me. I harbored not the slightest desire to either make him work for his money or nitpick his choices, but perhaps he didn't take it that way.

"Okay," he said with obvious annoyance as he put the car into gear, "*this* time I'm introducing you to one who's a sure thing!"

As he had before, he stopped the car at the entrance to a narrow street, but this time he had me get out of the car with him. Shoulder to shoulder, we climbed the stairs of an apartment building.

"This time," he said, knocking on the door, "it's a sure thing."

He pushed the woman who peered out at us back into the room and whispered something in her ear. I waited outside the doorway as he was doing this.

Hiro Boy returned to me

"She'll do fine."

The way he said it left no room for argument.

She was a rather large woman and not my type, but she was beautiful. I decided not to put Hiro Boy to any more trouble.

The woman brought out beer and set it on a coffee table, and Hiro Boy and I drank. After a while he left, leaving me and the woman in the apartment. A calendar printed in color hung on the wall. The face of the woman on the calendar was the same as the woman before me.

"Say, that's you!"

"That's right. I used to be a model."

After that, time passed in the expected fashion, and I headed home.

· 6 ·

"By the way," I said to Nao, "Hiro Boy fixed me up nicely that time. How are things working out for him?"

"He's happily married, more so each day."

That seemed like a curious response, so my response was intentionally vague.

"Ah . . . I see."

FAIR DALLIANCE

"He's really got himself a fine wife. But they're a strange couple."

I said nothing.

"You don't think so?"

"Well, I'm afraid I've never met his wife."

"Whoa, you didn't know?"

"Know what?"

"Hiro Boy introduced you to his own wife that time. You didn't know?"

I felt as if I'd been blind-sided.

"She was Hiro Boy's . . . ?"

"She certainly was. He does that sort of thing only rarely."

"Not such an admirable inclination, is it."

"It's not that odd an inclination . . . He sells his beloved wife to another man. He does a dramatic turn wherein he's a man who even does such a 'terrible' thing for the sake of the business."

"I see."

That's Hiro Boy for you.

Most certainly I didn't "get it." I recalled his face with fondness. But at the same time I also realized there was absolutely no way I could be a companion to Hiro Boy's narcissism.

The Flies

蠅

TRANSLATED BY LAWRENCE ROGERS

THE GIRL WAS BROUGHT up with great care. When she returned from school she was not permitted to go out again unless her parents knew exactly where she was going and how long she would be gone, and this was the case even after she became a high school student. She was an only daughter, so her father was especially strict with her.

The girl was the only one at home who was given her own room. Occasionally after she had gone to bed, something would be set loose within her. And then a kind of fire would suddenly burn at her core. When that happened the girl would get up, stand in front of her mirror, and take off her pajamas. She would be completely naked. Girls her age project a sense of good health, but they have a chubbiness into which a suggestion of stolidity is melded, and when that time has passed, it is often the case that the excess flesh gracefully disappears. In the case of this girl's nakedness, however, she had a lushness and roundness not consonant with her age.

The girl opened a desk drawer, took out lipstick that she had hidden at the back of the drawer, and lightly applied it to her lips to see what it would look like. Little by little she darkened the crimson on her lips. In the end her lips were almost garish in their redness.

By this time her areolas had swelled to small hillocks. She applied a touch of lipstick to one nipple and smudged it with her fingertips. She looked at this in the mirror for a while, then hastily wiped the lipstick off and stepped away from the mirror.

That day, after classes were over, there was a fellow in a student uniform waiting for her on the way home. The girl's high school was not coeducational. The young man had been a year ahead of her in middle school.

She was favorably disposed toward him. Previously letters from him had arrived at her house. The contents were not particularly untoward, but when her father heard of them he strictly forbade the correspondence.

After that the youth began waiting for her about once a week. He waited furtively behind the trunk of a large tree growing near a small man-made creek. By the time she reached the tree the students from her school were nowhere to be seen.

Her heart would beat faster when the tree came into view. And yet the two strolled on a path along the river for only some twenty minutes. Their conversation was meandering.

It was a hot and humid summer afternoon.

The girl had a well-proportioned body, with long, slender legs. That notwithstanding, from time to time she would stumble and stagger. She would suddenly lose her balance even when walking on flat and level ground. Their conversation was, as usual, meandering, but there were times when the atmosphere was strained; suddenly it was so dense it seemed a concentrate. In that instant the girl staggered and fell half a pace behind. As she steadied herself she saw before her the youth's uniformed back. And on that expanse she saw something extraordinary.

A mass of flies, the lower half of their bodies a glistening blue-green, covered the whole of his back. Their color was such that it looked as though someone had applied luminous paint to them. Their outsides were smooth, and yet to her eyes it seemed as though a sticky liquid compressed within them was oozing out of every single fly.

The color left her body. Yet again she lost her footing on some stones.

"What's wrong?" the youth asked, looking back at her.

"I stumbled again."

"What's to be done with you?" he muttered, laughing.

The girl began to avoid the youth after that.

THE BATTLE OF THE CLAYS

粘土合戦

TRANSLATED BY LAWRENCE ROGERS

I HATE THE SAUCE we put on pork cutlets in Japan, preferring instead Worcestershire sauce, but I didn't know what Worcestershire meant. I tried looking up the word printed on the sauce bottle in an English dictionary, but there was nothing. Once, when I was watching a quiz program on TV, they asked the question: "What's the meaning of the word 'Worcestershire' in Worcestershire sauce?" The answer was that it's the name of a town in England, where the sauce was first made.

Encyclopedic knowledge doesn't impress me, but in the case of Worcestershire sauce, I felt something that had been stuck in my craw for many years suddenly give way. Another imponderable still a puzzle for me is one of the words indicating weight class in boxing, "welter." I don't even know how it's spelled in English. There are indications that this mutual pummeling by two men called modern boxing, which developed during the pioneering era in America, at bottom recognizes only the heavyweight class as real boxing. The so-called lightweight class is on the heavy side in Japan. The English word *light* means just that, light as opposed to heavy, but when you get to the lighter classes in boxing, the names given them would seem to reflect more than weight differences. The junior flyweight class, in which the Japanese boxer Gushiken[1]

---

1 Gushiken Yōkō (b. 1955) was WBA light flyweight champion from 1976 to 1981.

is currently world champion, was originally called the mosquito class. Above flyweight, in ascending order, are bantamweight—*chabo* in Japanese—and featherweight, that is, *hane*. I don't know what welter is. I've asked all sorts of people about it but have gotten no reply.

In the meantime I've been hoping it would be a question on one of the quiz programs, but it may be too difficult.

But I watch quiz programs not just for that, but because I like them. I'm a special fan of Channel 10's "Panel Quiz."[2]

A rectangular board is divided vertically and horizontally into five rows and columns, forming on the board a total of twenty-five small rectangles. There are four chairs: white, red, green and blue, and a contestant sits at each. When a contestant answers correctly, he can make one of the small rectangles on the board his color. I'll pass over the finer points of the rules, but let's say that one of the rows or columns has the four colors in a row: red, white, blue and green. If the last panel, next to the green one, is taken by red, the three colors that find themselves between the two red rectangles are then all changed to red. They would seem to have taken a page from the Othello Game—also originating in Japan—so if you know the rules for it, this game is easy enough to understand. Depending on how many rectangles one captures, it's possible to turn the board all red, all white, all blue, or solid green.

I'd been watching the program as I lay in bed. The green, caught between red, turned red, and the red changed into blue; the four colors on the board were transformed into other colors, and then the game was over. I stretched out an arm and flicked off the TV, stretched out face up on the bed and waited for sleep to come.

It was the middle of the day. I'd been bedridden and hadn't been able to sleep for two weeks. Again and again I'd direct my gaze at the clock, to see each time that about ten minutes had

2 TV Asahi's popular *Panel Quiz Attack 25*, currently the longest running quiz show on Japanese television, hosted for 36 years by the late Kodama Kiyoshi.

gone by. The passage of time in each interval was precisely the same. People who complain they can't sleep, though they may not be aware of it themselves, repeatedly fall into brief, fitful sleep. At that time, however, I looked at the clock six times an hour, 144 times a day, then went on to the next day to begin all over again. It did not seem to me that sleep descended upon me at any time.

You can't expect, however, a human being to survive without any sleep whatsoever day after day. When one's limit is reached, the defense mechanism within the body begins to function, and one can then go to sleep. Since that thought first came to me almost half a month had passed.

Suddenly, on the TV screen I saw the game board, divided into its twenty-five rectangles. The set had to be off, and the program, less than thirty minutes long, was already over. The red in the upper right-hand panel, like a very viscous glue, began to slowly flow down onto and over the blue panel directly beneath it. The blue exuded itself onto a green panel at a bottom corner, and the green paint at the top of the board became a thick stratum of green clay, attempting to stem and repel the flow of exuded blue that was oozing toward it. As blue and green fought each other, from the boundary between the contending colors a human hand slithered out from the board, all five fingers shaking furiously, the flat of the hand opening and closing. As this was happening, the entire board was shaking back and forth.

The battle of the colors was breaking out all over, and other things were happening: a leg would suddenly project itself from the middle of the board as far as the knee, and in the upper left-hand corner something round would appear, apparently the elbow of a fully flexed arm. Each time this would happen, the board would sway to and fro.

As all this was going on my body was bouncing up and down on the bed, a sensation that continued for some time. I tore myself off of my bed and stood on the floor.

"This is a dream," I told myself.

Sweat poured from my body. I opened the bedroom door and went into the bathroom, immediately to the left, and wiped the sweat off myself with a bath towel. I'd also been unable to eat, as well as sleep, so I was unsteady on my feet. I sat down on the toilet, head down.

"Yet that sort of thing," I heard a voice say, "is entirely possible."

Where else could the voice be coming from but me? Yet it had the sound and tone of a commentator on social phenomena.

"That," it intoned, "is a mob, an audience angry at television. Their dissatisfaction is the dissatisfaction of people who have been called together early in the morning for an audience participation show, only to be kept waiting hours, and for a program that lasts less than thirty minutes. Their ill-feeling is toward a TV station which told them they shouldn't complain because they were going to put them on the program."

I wiped the sweat off my body again and returned to my bed, towel in hand, and lay down. Suddenly my body began to shake up and down again. On the TV screen the battle between the colors continued. As the shaking of my body grew more intense, the picture on the screen changed.

It was a rather large clearing in the woods. Seven or eight men and women were causing a commotion of some sort. There was a cloth curtain between two long bamboo poles. The men, two supporting each pole, went off, one pair to the left, another to the right. The curtain between the two poles became fully taut. On the curtain were drawn twenty-five squares exactly like those on the earlier quiz show board. They were painted in four different colors. The group that had gathered was dressed so lightly as to appear to be wearing little more than underclothes. Some of the women wore *happi* coats. The men's shirts and what seemed to be long underwear were utterly filthy, coated with paint and dirt.

The men holding the bamboo poles began to move them up and down, at which the curtain began to undulate, and the entire group started shouting in unison to keep time.

"Wasshoi! Wasshoi!"

The scene turned halfway round like a revolving stage, and my gaze shifted to behind the undulating curtain. There were several men and women there, each with a can of paint in one hand and a brush in the other. Their brushes dripping with any color they fancied, they slapped paint on the back of the curtain, and the color soaked into it. Now and then one of the men would leap into the air and throw himself against it. The curtain would rip, and his arms and feet would thrust themselves through the front of it.

Once again the stage revolved halfway, and the board came into view. The colors had at each other, and from time to time hands and legs protruded from the curtain.

I shook my head vigorously and forced my torso up off the bed once again.

"This is a dream."

Sweat rolled down my forehead. I wiped it away with the bath towel.

I again heard the voice intoning in the fashion of the cultural commentator.

"These things really happen. Right now cameramen from other TV stations are rushing to the scene. Details will soon be broadcast in special news bulletins."

My position was a busy one. I was a spectator, I was a person who was privy to what was going on backstage, and I was being provided with commentary.

And all of this oppressed me with an intense sense of reality. I had switched off the TV set, but I had the feeling that if I turned it back on and changed the channel, I would most certainly see special news bulletins before me on the screen.

But the strength had ebbed from my arms, and I made no attempt to move. I fell across the bed; my body began shaking again.

The clearing in the middle of the forest again came into view. The filth from the paint and the mud was worse than before. A woman rolled on the ground, in a frenzy of excitement perhaps, her body caking itself with mud. The poles rose and fell violently, and the curtain undulated.

The rhythmic shouts erupted skyward.

"Wasshoi! Wasshoi!"

Men and women came running out of the woods from all directions.

"A festival! A festival!" they all shouted, gamboling into the clearing. Several men immediately clutched at the bamboo poles. The taut curtain quivered all the more violently.

"A festival! A festival!"

The number of people grew endlessly. Only the taut curtain shook above the swirl of people, the men holding the poles disappearing from view.

"This is how a mob forms," said the commentator-style voice, and I returned to reality.

I got up again and sat on the side of the bed, slowly wiping the sweat from my body with the bath towel. I looked at the clock. The hands indicated it was 3:10.

The quiz program had ended at 1:40, so an hour and a half had passed.

"Was it a nightmare?" I muttered.

For the first time in half a month, however, I had not been looking at the clock every ten minutes.

A nightmare is most certainly sleep of a sort, but is it really rest?

Katsushika Ward

葛飾

Translated by Lawrence Rogers

· 1 ·

Talking to a visitor about work, I found myself unable to maintain the sitting position I was in.

"Excuse me for a moment."

I lay down on the front room sofa.

"I'm comfortable when my head and feet are at the same level," I said as I went from lying on my side to lying face down. Breathing was shallow and easier when I did that.

"And I'm uncomfortable watching you," Sasaki, my visitor, said.

His words could have been sarcastic, in which case there was nothing I could say. But sarcasm was apparently not his intent.

"My mother had lumbago, and for three years there wasn't a doctor who could help her, but she was cured with just one treatment session. A year's gone by, but she's had no relapse."

"What sort of treatment?"

"They call it shiatsu, or maybe osteopathy, or . . . oh yeah, chiro . . ."

"Chiropractic. You mean chiropractic."

"Right, right."

"Where was her doctor?"

"Katsushika."

"Katsushika?" I parroted. There were two considerations here for me.

It would doubtless take considerable time to go from my home at the far edge of Setagaya Ward to Katsushika Ward. You could say I would be going from one end of Tokyo to the other.

Second, I remembered that Shibamata in Katsushika was the home base of Tora-san in the movie series which has as its central character the miscreant Tora.

I was naturally surprised when Marilyn Monroe was still alive and active and I heard there were Americans who had never heard of her. Now I probably have to briefly explain who Tora is. As for his work, he is pretty much a grifter who sells his goods with a flamboyant spiel, on the road in his crepe shirt and wool bellyband. His only sister helps their uncle's family, which runs a dumpling shop in Shibamata. Tora loves this younger sister, and from time to time he ambles back when it suits him.

"Hey, I'm back. I'm home now, so there's nothin' to worry about," Tora says cheerfully. "Everybody can relax."

The expression on the faces of his relatives turns sour. That is because whenever he returns it's one problem after another, a slough of worry.

"Katsushika . . . that's where Tora is."

"Right. When you see that movie in the *shitamachi* area— the old part of Tokyo—you'll find audience response interesting."

"You don't say. In what way?"

Sasaki's answer was intentionally obscure.

"Tora, whatever else you might say, is a character who evokes sharp distinctions between subjective and objective. Therein lies the uneasiness of the older women of the *shitamachi*. You can hear them: 'Tora's a loser. Look! Look! He's at it again!'"

"I see what you mean. That's what's good about the Katsushika and Senju areas, isn't it. Not to change the subject, but as for the doctor, it's a fact that you can have lumbago or a strained back and the like cured with one session of osteopathy. But I wonder how it'll go with my problem."

"How will it go, indeed?"

"These days some people think the Japanese constitution may not be suited to Western medicine. I intend to try Eastern medicine or traditional Chinese remedies for a year. I've already stopped taking Western medication for some months. I wonder if you might ask if they'll take my case and introduce me."

· 2 ·

Sasaki phoned several days later.

"The doctor I talked to said an affliction like yours can be taken care of in one go-round. And as someone to treat, they would welcome a famous patient who came to them."

"I'm famous, am I?"

"You fall into that category, right? Of course, now that you mention it, yours is not a name that has wide currency."

"What was his response?"

"Nothing in particular."

"Well, I say that's good. And when can I go?"

"He said in three weeks. In any case, he said they're busy and can't take on new patients. You're to be an exception."

"Waiting three weeks is an exception, is it? Which is to say, it's another twenty one days!"

"Their pace is a bit leisurely, isn't it."

"As it stands now I've no other options, so please do what you can."

"He said to come by 1 p.m. the day of your appointment," Sasaki said, then hung up.

· 3·

I arrived on the appointed day, taking the train and the bus. It took me close to three hours, no doubt because my choice of lines was inept, but I got there at the agreed-upon 1 p.m., if only barely.

The gilt letters on the glass front door of the small wood-frame house said "Laboratory for the Adjustment of the Torso and Extremities." Shoes and sandals lay where they had been stepped out of on the narrow entryway floor; from there one could see everything inside the building. Four beds were lined up in an area that had wooden flooring, and on these men and women were lying face up. On tatami mats raised higher than the wooden flooring two men, stripped to the waist and in red and navy blue sweatpants, lay face up doing stretches. With the assistance of men and women wearing white doctors' gowns they would momentarily arch their bodies, then drop them with great force onto the tatami, slamming their thighs against it, first to the left, then to the right, their knees sharply bent.

"Go on!" the white-coated assistants called out, "Harder!"

I had assumed shiatsu or osteopathy and the like were gentler sorts of therapies. As I stood there on the concrete floor at the entryway, staring blankly at all this, a woman in a white smock approached. When I gave her Sasaki's name, she nodded ambiguously and held out to me a new-patient form.

"Please wait there," she said, pointing to several wooden chairs lined up against the wall on the wooden floor area.

I sat down on a chair, and when I had finished filling out the slip of paper, the woman took it to an old man sitting at a small desk at the back of the room.

The old man in a white smock was, of course, the director. Perhaps he was close to seventy; he was lean, but his posture was good and suggested he was vigorous. He was saying something without looking at the piece of paper. The woman took out a medical chart and began filling it out.

There were some ten patients. After they had done close to twenty minutes of rigorous exercises on the tatami, some of them moved to the beds. Cords were coiled around their wrists and ankles; it was apparently some sort of electrotherapy.

From time to time the phone would ring. Receiver to her ear, the female assistant would call to the back of the room.

"Sir, it's a new patient."

"Out of the question for now."

His shrill reply was immediate, his tone harsh, but in the end he would approve an examination for three weeks later.

Now and again the door would open and a new patient would come in. You could certainly say the practice was flourishing, but, it seemed, not to the extent that there should be a good three-week wait. Considerable time went by, but my name wasn't called; I was still sitting in my chair.

A little before three the old director stood up and approached. However, he passed right by me and went out the door. He was carrying a small cloth-wrapped bundle. When he returned some fifteen minutes later he went to the tatami area and worked with a patient sitting there, vigorously pulling up on one arm.

It was well past four p.m. Already three and a half hours had gone by. A good number of patients who had come after me had been treated already and left. It was a long wait, surrounded entirely by the faces of first-timers, and I was uncomfortable.

"Well now," the old director said, turning toward me and directing his gaze over the top of his glasses. He looked at my chart and said the name written on it.

"It's a name I've heard before, I think."

The eyes of all the other patients focussed on me as one, but their gaze was blank and they gave no response. When he had satisfied himself that he knew it, he once again uttered the name on the chart.

"Y'know . . . it's a famous name. It was in a weekly magazine the other day."

Curiosity flitted across the faces of the patients, but otherwise their expressions remained blank.

Had I been on display for three and a half hours? I hadn't been that effective an exhibit, and you might say I was shopworn goods. Perhaps that had been the old man's strategy since getting Sasaki's phone call.

"All right," the woman assistant said, "please change."

When she opened the corner curtain of the tatami room, I saw three rattan baskets lined up in the narrow space, and in them were bedraggled sweatpants, their colors faded.

"Do I take off my shirt too?" I asked, poking my head out from behind the curtain.

Women patients were being treated with their blouses on.

"Of course," I heard the old man say, his tone peremptory.

There were always patients in groups of two in the tatami room and the assistants, male and female, treating them. The old director's function was guidance, though he involved himself occasionally.

When I was supine on the tatami the male assistant by me muttered.

"Oh, you've no skin."

That was true, but it hadn't occurred to me to put it that way. It was as though someone had taken a pin frog used in flower arranging and rubbed raw the skin all over my body. The skin on my face was the same. Only the skin from my throat to my chest was smooth. There it was as though melanin had settled in like daubed *sumi* ink.

"According to Sasaki," I ventured, "this will clear up with one session."

I had little faith in that myself, but there is such a thing as unexpected good luck.

"Listen," the old director said, his speech fitful, "that's different from lumbago, you know. For something like that, just

— 160 —

one visit is out of the question. I'd say . . . it'll take two or three . . . for sure."

The old director grabbed hold of the flesh on my shoulder and pulled one arm up. His pull was sharp and strong, and it was something that made me believe in him. The season was early spring and the light had already dimmed. The day would be coming to an end by the time I arrived home. I got an appointment for the following week and returned home, taking almost three hours to get there.

· 4 ·

I awoke the next day feeling hopeful, but my symptoms had not improved in the slightest.

A week later, to the contrary, they had worsened.

Should I go one more time, after all?

The day of the appointment I decided to drive myself. I still heard that voice in my ear: *Oh, you've no skin.* And it had been quite unpleasant on the train, concerned as I was about many of my fellow passengers staring at me.

A twenty-minute drive from my home near the Futako Tamagawa amusement center, I took Loop Route Seven, and after that I entrusted the car to the broad highway. Looking at the map, I could see that this, after all, was the only way to go. I could also have used the expressway, but with congestion appropriate to its being renamed an All Automobiles highway, it would be six of one and half a dozen of the other; moreover, it's nothing but trouble after you get off the expressway.

Coming to the end of Loop Route Seven, I turned left and was right at the overpass at Kamiuma, where I passed under National Highway 246. A good while back when there was construction going on, it often took close to twenty minutes to get through. The work went on for some three years; during that period I was often forced to drive through there.

When you pass Daita in Setagaya Ward, at its intersection with the Kōshū Highway, you're at an area well-known as a traffic congestion zone. You take a hard right across Kōshū Highway and you're in Suginami Ward. Passing Hōnan-chō, you finally cross the Ōme Highway. A little while after you pass under the large railway overpass in Kōenji, you run through Nakano Ward and, exiting Maruyama-chō near Saginomiya, you immediately enter Nerima Ward.

Passing along the Toyotama Overpass, where it crosses Jūsangen Road, you're at Hazawa-chō, but there's a lot of congestion there, too. But it wasn't a problem now. To be confined in a car, just by oneself, and move along at a snail's pace is how life is these days; or to put it another way, it's proof that one is alive. As to why I'm able to carry out the task of driving a car, the tension I feel gripping the steering wheel stimulates the adrenal glands and adrenaline is secreted. This adrenaline is effective in dealing with my illness and, at the least, it allows me to continue driving. Beyond that it has no effect.

Some years back the congestion hereabouts annoyed me no end. A woman I knew lived some 500 meters off this boulevard. It took forever for the car to get to where she lived. That's not the case now. When I stopped for the red light on the way, as I remember it, I turned my head and looked down the street. Of course there was no way I could see the house from there.

I would meet with her, parking my car near her house. I met her again and again, visiting on the average once a week, and I didn't phone her the rest of the time. I think it's fair to say that given this situation it would be inconceivable that a woman would not look about for another man. And when she had another man the signs were there; that's the sort of woman she was. Normally her skin was smooth and tawny, but at those times her whole body was wrapped in a gray membrane, and the tips of her fingers were tacky. No doubt loathing was at work in her heart, yet the loathing may have been directed at the woman herself. Or, who knows? A carelessness steals into the junctures between acts atop a bed. When she continued to feign ignorance at such times, the viscosity at some point would leave her skin and her actions reverted to what they had been before.

I praised her sexuality. "You're really good."

"That's because I do it with passion," she shot back at me, her tone almost angry.

In the end she got married. It happened a some time ago. And yet she would still phone, as though it was something she just remembered to do. About once a year. There had been a call from her a little earlier.

"How are you? Take care of yourself, okay? No need for you to work. Stay alive, okay?"

Her words sounded spiteful, as though she had detected the terrible condition I was in.

"You sound really weak. You're not doing any work, are you. You intend to go on living?"

But was it only this kind of simple ill will alone that lingered in her? I hung up, consoling myself that she was no doubt feeling more than one emotion.

When I passed Hazawa-chō I was in Itabashi Ward, and soon at the intersection with the Kawazoe highway, and when I'd gone by that there was another intersection, this one with Nakasendō. It was not far, but it took a long time to get to Kita Ward.

Passing under the railway overpass of the Akabane line, I then crossed over the long bridge that spans the Tōhoku, Jōetsu and Shin'etsu lines. From the car window I could see countless rails running parallel into the distance. That was Kita Ward, and when I crossed over the Shinkamiya bridge, which is where the last Kamiya-chō sign is, I was in Adachi Ward. Under the bridge is the Sumida River; I soon saw the Shikahama bridge, which spans the broader Arakawa River.

Loop Route Seven takes up a good deal of space in Adachi Ward. The number of buildings on both sides of the road in Shikahama and Kōhoku decline as you go along, but the amount of traffic doesn't. Skirting West Araidaishi, I pass

Yanaka, close by Umejima, Aoi, and Ayase, and the cloverleaf at the Nikkō Highway, at last coming to an end at the Jōban line in Kameari; this is Katsushika Ward.

The Laboratory for the Adjustment of the Torso and Extremities was nearby.

From time to time I had looked at the dashboard clock as I drove. Although I had passed through seven wards, it was a distance I could have driven in about forty minutes if it had been late at night. In the daytime, however, the roads are in chaos, so it took me three hours and fifteen minutes.

· 5 ·

It was past one in the afternoon when I arrived. I was prepared to be kept waiting three and a half hours this day as well.

Around two a young man entered.

"*Sensei*, I've brought some mugwort rice cakes." His tone was informal as he handed the older man a paper package.

"Oh, thanks. Mugwort's already growing?"

"Right. These're home-made cakes. Picked the mugwort on the embankment."

"They're one of my favorites," the old man said, opening the package then and there and biting into the pale green rice cakes. He picked up another.

"Would you like to have one?" he asked, sticking it under my nose.

"Oh, thanks."

I accepted it and began eating, but it felt odd eating in a building where there were so many patients.

Close to three the old man, as he had done before, hurriedly left, cloth bundle in hand.

"Gonna be late! Gonna be late!"

"*Sensei*'s off to the bank again?" the young man who had brought the rice cakes asked an assistant with a laugh. You could tell from the way he asked he didn't expect an answer.

Now that I thought about it, the fee for treatment was on the high side. If your complaint cleared up in one session, it would not be that expensive, of course, but if not . . .

To my surprise I was summoned to the tatami room after the rice-cake man had been treated and left.

"How do you feel?" the old director asked.

"Not that much better, really."

"I supposed as much. That's often the case. You've gotten worse, if anything, in reaction to the treatment. That'll be taken care of when we get all of the toxins out of you."

That sort of expression one frequently heard from dispensers of folk remedies, so when I heard it I began to lose heart. Actually, I'd already lost a good deal of heart.

The old director jerked hard on my feet.

"I'd guess that's the case. Two or three more sessions should do it. Today, later, we'll try electrotherapy," he said, directing his gaze at a bed in the room with the wood flooring.

A male patient lying on one of the beds asked him a question.

"Sir, is this like an electric massager?"

"R–Ridiculous!"

The old director had a long, lean face, and several tufts of down-like hair grew on his head. He glared at the patient through his glasses, his face flushing as he answered.

"That's a . . . it's much more . . . it's very high class."

"I'm pressed for time today, so . . ."

I was begging off with a fabrication, and the old man was obviously dissatisfied.

"That can't be helped. Well, we'll do it next time. There's something wrong with your colon. It's releasing toxins."

His pat response, yet again.

"However, let's see, you'll have two or three more sessions. Let me give you this."

He handed me an appointment card for five days later.

"Will I feel like coming then?" I asked myself as I left the building.

· 6 ·

The home of a famous master of chiropractic was a five-minute walk from my house. I'd not yet seen the building, but I'd heard that when you went into the entryway Beethoven's Ninth Symphony would be thundering forth. It was said the master sat in the large examination room on a dais raised above the rest of the room, the relationship between him and the patient as between the founder of a religion and a follower. He had about him the air of a doctor who serves the Imperial Household, and I understand the social position of his patients was the highest and that you paid a hefty fee to enroll as a patient. Several people I know recommended I go see him.

There are certain types of illnesses that are cured by becoming a believer. This, however, was not that sort of affliction, nor is my personality the sort that lends itself to belief. I declined each time they made their recommendation.

That being the situation, why had I set off for Katsushika? A drowning man clutches at straws. Was that my state of mind? If it's the same straw in both cases, isn't five minutes on foot closer than three hours by car?

The master in Katsushika was quite arrogant and doubtless also thought of himself as the founder of a religion. The "founder's" intent to be so and his lack of the makings thereof was certainly interesting, but my interest alone would not cure me.

Even now I was in pain. After I bathed, the first time in quite a while, I curled up on the bed and thought about this. The taking of a bath is a religious austerity. I came out of the bath, but my body was wracked with pain until I stopped sweating. Curled up, I endured. That night I had washed my hair, so my suffering was twofold.

— 166 —

Comparing the pain with how it was before, I realized it had not eased in the slightest. This in spite of Sasaki telling me that there were instances of a cure after one treatment. No, I suspected the nature of the affliction was unique, which probably meant nothing could be done. In any event, there was no longer any point in setting off for Katsushika. It was about as meaningless as walking to the mansion of the famous master of chiropractic.

· 7 ·

It was toward the end of summer. That day as well I was traveling over Loop Route Seven in my car. I had put an air conditioner in the car. I'd been commuting to Katsushika several times every two weeks. I'd had fifty sessions, but there was not the slightest improvement in my condition. Yet even if I had confined myself to my home, I would still be simply lying in bed and watching television. What I was capable of doing now was simply sleeping and watching TV *and* driving my car.

I arrived in Katsushika in a little over three hours. I now brought pajama bottoms to avoid wearing the sweat pants they provided.

"How's it going, *Sensei*?" the old man called out to me. He had been calling me *sensei* for some time now. It rarely happens that a doctor will call a patient that. Which is to say, the old man was showing that he was an osteopath, not an osteopathic physician.

"*Sensei*, have you felt like working a little?"

"Really, I can't."

"It's a genuine puzzle, isn't it. Well, please come this way."

He opened the door at the back of the examination room. It led to a small room. Cards for writing calligraphy were stacked on the table inside.

What, again?

A month before I had confronted the same situation. That time I'd been handed a felt-tipped pen and written *Smiling with Adjustment of the Torso and Extremities.*

Doing calligraphy for people is anything but easy for me, and I usually turn down requests, but a patient is in a weak position. The old director had looked at my inept column of characters with a jaundiced eye.

"This time please just write the single character for 'longevity'," he said as he handed me a brush. I looked for the usual inkstone case, but there was just a can of *sumi* ink sitting on the desk. I was to write the specified sinograph on the twenty or so cards stacked there. I thought to myself as I wrote that these would doubtless serve as material evidence that I had been cured in one session. The old director was brimming to overflow with any number of stories of his brilliant record of therapy successes: how a certain large hospital was referring an endless succession of patients to him, making him incredibly busy, or how he cured—in one day—the liver problem of the younger brother of a well-known chanson singer.

"Today you're going at it really well." He was at my elbow encouraging me as I brushed the character on the cards.

"Oh, sorry, but let's write something else on that one, right in the middle," he said when I finally came to the last card.

"And what would you like me to write?"

"*Tsurukame Sushi.*"

"How's that?"

The old man took the brush and wrote the characters for *Tsurukame Sushi* on a miswritten calligraphy card that I had discarded on the tatami.

"What's that?"

"A sushi restaurant near here. I'm on friendly terms with them. The tuna there, I'll tell you, it's the best in Japan. Let's go there some time soon."

"Uh-huh . . . Well, I realized that's what it was, but you want me to write Tsurukame Sushi right in the middle of the card?"

"Exactly."

"I wonder if that's what you want. Isn't this supposed to be a dedication?"

"A dedication?"

"I mean, don't you want me to write it smaller and off to the side: *To the Owner of Tsurukame Sushi*?"

His response was immediate.

"No. Right in the middle and big," the elder said, his tone obstinate.

I was getting electricity on the bed those days. I would lie supine, cords wrapped around my wrists and ankles. The old director would turn the dials on a box-shaped device at the foot of the bed, eyeing a needle on a calibrated scale.

He inevitably began the procedure with the same injunction: "Tell me if you get a shock and I'll cut back on the electricity."

I'd lie there like that for an hour.

There was a window at the foot of the bed. Four rectangular frames containing what appeared to be certificates hung in a row on the wall above the window. There was one written only in English. I had known about these for weeks, but that day I had more than enough time to read the script on the pieces of paper.

In each case they were certificates of completion for osteopathy or shiatsu techniques. The document in English was issued by a chiropractic association in Japan. It was then that I suddenly noticed it. The dates the certificates were issued were all ten years earlier. If the old director was now seventy, that would mean he got them just ten years before. I had had the impression he'd been in this practice, and only this practice, since his youth.

What sort of life had he lived before he turned sixty? I cast a furtive glance at the old *sensei* as I recalled the sight of him hurriedly setting off for the bank just before it was about to close, cloth-wrapped bundle in hand. It was hot now, so he was wearing a crepe shirt and a *suteteko*, knee-length summer underwear. The rascally image of Tora-san imposed itself over him.

When the bed therapy was over and I was paying, a female assistant told me that hereafter I would be getting a twenty per cent discount off the fee.

"Oh, I am?" I said, paying the lesser amount.

I turned to the old *sensei.*

"So I should brace myself for a drawn-out struggle against this, after all?"

"A drawn-out struggle? Ridiculous! The very idea! You're almost finished."

The old director's response was indignant, but I had already been going there for six months.

· 8 ·

The congestion on the roads when I returned home that day was especially bad. Apparently there had been an accident and from time to time the lines of cars came to a standstill.

My condition that day was especially poor. My entire body was wracked with pain, as though tightly bound from front to back. I had stopped taking all of my Western-style medicine close to a year before. There is a medicine for my illness that is dramatically effective for a certain period of time. However, it had worrisome side effects, and I'd already taken a considerable amount of it over an extended period, so I wanted to try doing without it, and yet. . . .

The old *sensei* himself, having taken on a difficult patient, may well have been stumped by the case. I had the card for my next appointment in my pocket, but wouldn't it be kinder to not use it? Or perhaps, to the contrary, might he be angered by my not trusting him? I couldn't come to a conclusion on this point.

That was around the end of August, but I dragged out my trips to Katsushika to September tenth. There had been absolutely no change in my condition. And I had no idea what was in the old *sensei's* mind.

· 9 ·

My condition worsened at the beginning of November. So much so that even driving the car was too much for me.

I no longer had any choice. I switched back to the Western medical treatments that I had been receiving originally.

I sent a letter of apology to the old *sensei*. I'm not sure why I sent it. Harboring such a sentiment was perhaps part and parcel of the affliction.

Three years later.

The chiropractic *sensei* who had the mansion a five-minute walk from my house died. Soon after that word reached me that the Katsushika *sensei* had died. Both of them had been in their early seventies. The *sensei* with the mansion who acted in such an imperious fashion, might he have had the—what shall we call it?—the duty to at least have lived to eighty? I consider that the *sensei* in Katsushika was likewise obligated, and yet I've also come to feel he was not.

FURTHER READING

BOOKS

The Dark Room, John Bester, translator, Kodansha International, 1975.

Toward Dusk and Other Stories, Andrew Clare, translator, Kurodahan Press, 2011.

SHORT STORIES

"Sudden Shower" (Shūu), translated by Geoffrey Bownas, *Japan Quarterly*, vol. 19, no. 4, October–December, 1972, pp. 446–457.

"Are the Trees Green?" (Kigi wa midori ka), translated by Adam Kabat, *The Shōwa Anthology: Modern Japanese Short Stories, 1929–1984*, Van C. Gessel and Tomone Matsumoto, editors, Kodansha International, 1985, pp. 146–168.

"In Akiko's Room" (Shōfu no heya), translated by Howard Hibbett, *Contemporary Japanese Literature: An Anthology of Fiction, Film and Other Writing Since 1945*, Howard Hibbett, editor, Alfred A. Knopf, 1977, pp. 401–411.

"Birds, Beasts, Insects and Fish" (Chōjūchūgyo), translated by Maryellen Toman Mori, *Japan Quarterly*, vol. 28, no. 1, January–March 1981, pp. 91–102.

"Scenes at Table" (Shokutaku no kōkei), translated by Geraldine Harcourt, *Japan Echo*, vol. 12, 1985, pp. 42–45.

"Personal Baggage" (Kaban no nakami), translated by John Bester, *Japanese Literature Today*, no. 1, March 1976, pp. 4–8.

"Three Policemen" (Sannin no keikan), translated by Hugh Clarke, *Seven Stories of Modern Japan*, Leith Morton, editor, University of Sydney East Asian Series number 5, Wild Peony, 1991, pp. 51–56.

Permissions

Grateful acknowledgment is made to the publications where the following stories were first published in English.

"Hydrangeas" (紫陽花) is reprinted from *Zyzzyva*, vol. 3, no. 2, Summer 1987, pp. 114–125.

"The Battle of the Clays" (粘土合戦) is reprinted from *The East*, vol. 25, no. 3, September–October 1989, pp. 23–25.

"I Ran Over a Cat" (猫踏んじゃった) is reprinted from *Chelsea 50*, 1991, pp. 90–97.

"Something Unexpected" (不意の出来事) is reprinted from *Chelsea 58*, 1995, pp. 118–131.

Initial Japanese publication of stories is as follows:

"My Bed Is a Boat" (寝台の舟) first published in *Bungakukai*, vol. 12, no. 12, December, 1958.

"Japanese Handball" (手鞠) first published in *Shinchō*, vol. 56, no. 11, November, 1959.

"On Houses" (家屋について) first published in *Shinchō*, vol. 58, no. 7, July, 1961.

"The Man Who Fired the Bath" (風呂焚く男) first published in *Bungei*, vol. 1, no. 5, July, 1962.

"Perfume Bottles" (香水瓶) first published in *Chi·Kōsuibin*, Gakushū Kenkyūsha, May, 1964.

"The Illusionist" (手品師) first published in *Chi·Kōsuibin*, Gakushū Kenkyūsha, May, 1964.

"Hydrangeas" (紫陽花) first published in *Fūkei*, vol. 5, no. 11, November, 1964.

"I Ran Over a Cat" (猫踏んじゃった) first published in *Shōsetsu Shinchō*, vol. 19, no. 1, January, 1965.

"Something Unexpected" (不意の出来事) first published in *Bungakukai*, vol. 19, no. 4, April, 1965.

"Three Dreams" (夢三つ) first published in *Ōru Yomimono*, vol. 21, no. 4, April, 1966.

"Twins" (雙生) first published in *Shinchō*, vol. 63, no. 5, May, 1966.

"A Certain Married Couple" (ある夫婦) first published in *Shōsetsu Shinchō*, vol. 21, no. 1, January, 1967.

"The Flies" (蠅) first published in *Gunzō*, vol. 26, no. 1, January, 1971.

"The Battle of the Clays" (粘土合戦) first published in *Yasei Jidai*, vol. 5, no. 1, January, 1978.

"Katsushika Ward" (葛飾) first published in *Gunzō*, vol. 35, no. 1, January, 1980.

About the Translators

Lawrence Rogers is emeritus professor of Japanese at the Hilo campus of the University of Hawai'i and editor of the anthology *Tokyo Stories: A Literary Stroll*, recipient of the 2004 translation award from the Donald Keene Center of Japanese Culture, Columbia University.

Hiroko Igarashi teaches Japanese at the University of Hawai'i at Hilo campus.

William Matsuda is a Ph.D. candidate at the University of Hawai'i at Manoa currently doing research in Kyoto, Japan.

About the Artist

Kyōsuke Tchinai (智内兄助) was born in 1948 in Ehime, Japan. In 1966, he graduated from Imabari-Nishi high school, and entered the National University of Fine Arts. He received several distinguished awards including The Prize for Excellence at the young Japanese Painters' Exhibition, 1988, and The Yasui Award, 1991. From 1981 onwards, he participated in large group exhibitions such as The Cleveland Biennial (USA), the Ueno-no-Mori Grand Prix Exhibition (Japan), and the Yasui Award Exhibition (Japan).

Since 1983, he has held major solo exhibitions at the Tokyo Central Art Museum, the Kitakata Museum, Japan, the Kuma Museum, the Nakata Museum, Takashimaya and the Ehime Fine Arts Museum. In 2000, he signed an exclusive worldwide contract with the Tamenaga Gallery, which has already organized two solo exhibitions in their Paris gallery. The works of Tchinai are kept in many Japanese museums (Aichi, Imabari, Saitama, Kariya, etc.) as well as in private collections, including that of Baroness Ariane de Rothschild.

CPSIA information can be obtained at www.ICGtesting.com
Printed in the USA
BVOW020552220312

285765BV00001B/5/P